TRIGGER JUSTICE

DATE DUE

MAR 3 1 2002	
SEP 5 2003	
SEP 2 2 2006	
NOV 0 8 2006	

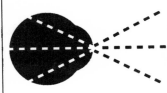

TRIGGER JUSTICE

Leslie Ernenwein

WHEELER
PUBLISHING

Published in 2003 by arrangement with Golden West Literary Agency.

Wheeler Large Print Western Series.

The text of this Large Print edition is unabridged.
Other aspects of the book may vary from the original edition.

Set in 16 pt. Plantin by Al Chase.

Printed in the United States on permanent paper.

Library of Congress Cataloging-in-Publication Data

Ernenwein, Leslie.
    Trigger justice : (rebels ride proudly) / by Leslie Ernenwein.
        p. cm.
    ISBN 1-58724-388-1 (lg. print : sc : alk. paper)
    1. Large type books.   I. Title.
PS3555.R58 T7 2003
    813'.54—dc21   2002193392

To
SLIM
who shared the Shack of Dreams

1. Tall and Tough

This was late autumn with Tonto Flats turned tawny by sun-cured grama grass. Mesquite beans in the thickets along Commissary Creek were brittle dry, so that the slightest breeze set them to rattling. It occurred to Jeff Tennant that the beans were the exact ivory color they'd been the last time he crossed this creek and that the same wheel-scarred boulders protruded above the water here at the ford. While his sorrel gelding drank leisurely, Tennant recalled the occasion of that crossing three years ago. He had been driving his first beef gather to Quadrille, twenty fat steers bearing his Roman Four brand. . . .

A whimsical smile loosened Tennant's lips, changing his angular face and giving it a youthfulness that was in keeping with his twenty-eight years. But the smile didn't change his gray eyes; it didn't touch them at all.

"Three years," he said. He cursed, and built a cigarette, and said again, "Three years."

So sitting, with the brim of his sweat-stained hat cuffed back and his long black hair merging with the four-day stubble of whiskers that shagged his jaws, Jeff Tennant looked like a saddle tramp. He wore a faded cotton shirt which had once been blue; his riding pants showed bachelor patches in both knees and his brush-scabbed boots had run-over heels. But his gun belt and holster were new, the tooled leather store yellow and store stiff.

When his horse finished drinking Tennant rode on across the ford; he was topping the north bank when a girl rode out of the brush so near that he recognized her at once as being Leona Bell, whose father owned one of the two large ranches in Bunchgrass Basin. Tennant discarded his cigarette; he showed her a frugal courtesy by nudging his hat brim, and said, "Howdy, ma'am."

Leona Bell nodded acknowledgement. She halted her horse and sat with both gloved hands on saddle horn in the contemplative fashion of a cattle buyer calculating the weight of a steer. Sunlight gave her brown eyes an amber shine; her jet-black hair, showing beneath the brim of a gray Stetson, accentuated the pallor of a composed, cameo-smooth face that now had an up-chinned tilt, so that she seemed to be looking down at him.

Tennant thought, *She always was prouder than seven peacocks,* and recalled that she had attended a fashionable Eastern school. Now, he guessed, she was showing him how folks in Bunchgrass Basin treated an ex-convict. . . .

A devil-be-damned grin creased Tennant's stubbled cheeks. He said brashly, "Take a good look," and, deliberately regarding the curves of her body, added, "While I do the same."

He thought that would end her silence. And her appraisal. But it didn't. She glanced at his new gun gear, at the sack of provisions tied behind his saddle, and at the brand on the bronc's left shoulder. Finally she asked, "Just riding through?"

Tennant understood now that she hadn't recognized him. Which seemed peculiar, until he remembered how few times they'd met and how casual those meetings were, for the Bells had never been overly sociable with folks who lived in the Tailholt Hills.

"Well?" she asked with cool arrogance.

"Make any difference to you, one way or the other?" Tennant inquired.

"Perhaps."

She considered him for a moment longer before asking, "Are you as tough as you look?"

"Yeah," Tennant told her, not smiling nor changing the brash tone of his voice. "I'm so tough I scare myself, almost."

She still sat with her gloved hands on the saddle horn and with the same up-chinned tilt to her head. But now there was a reflective expression in her eyes that made them seem less arrogant. "I could use a tough man," she announced.

"So?" Tennant prompted, more curious than he cared to reveal.

"Ever hear of the Bar Bell outfit?" she asked, and when he nodded, she said, "I'm boss of Bar Bell. I'm looking for a ramrod."

What, Tennant wondered, had happened to her father, and to Jules Huffmeyer, the crusty old ramrod who'd threatened to shoot any Tailholt Hills cowman caught slow-elking Bar Bell beef?

"Are you interested?" Leona asked.

Tennant shook his head.

"I'll pay your price," she offered.

Tennant said flatly, "You haven't got my price," and saw swift anger have its way with her.

She leaned forward in saddle, her right hand reaching out as if to grasp his sleeve. "Why?" she demanded. "Why won't you work for me?"

All her cool aloofness vanished. It was as if some inward heat warmed her eyes and stained her cheeks, giving her face an intense, graphic beauty that surprised Jeff Tennant. It lasted for only a moment, the warmth fading from her eyes as swiftly as it had come; but in that brief interval Tennant understood that there was this capacity for passion beneath the thin shield of her aloofness. He was tempted to tell her his name. She would know then why he wouldn't work for Bar Bell, or for any other outfit in Bunchgrass Basin. But all he said was, "I've got reasons aplenty."

Then he rode past her, put his horse to a run and quartered toward the Tailholt Hills.

For upwards of five minutes, while Leona Bell watched him ride off, she sat her horse in frowning silence. Afterward she crossed the creek and saw where fresh hoof prints entered the road from the west, and said thoughtfully, "So Mister Tall and Tough didn't come through Quadrille."

10

She was wondering about that, and about his "reasons aplenty," when she rode into Quadrille and put up her horse at McGonigle's Livery. There was, she decided, only one reason a trail tramp would detour around town: he didn't want to be seen. So thinking, she crossed Main Street and spoke to Sheriff Sam Lambert who sat in the stippled shade of a pepper tree on the jail side of the courthouse.

"I want to look at your rogue's gallery," she informed him and went into the office.

Lambert rose from his chair with an old man's reluctance; he said, "They ain't much to look at," and propelled his saddle-warped boots to the doorway.

Leona peered at the half-dozen fly-specked posters on the bulletin board, seeing at once that none of them closely resembled the man she'd met at Commissary Creek. Then she glanced at Lambert's disordered desk and asked, "Any new circulars you haven't posted?"

"No," Sheriff Sam said, eyeing her in a speculative fashion. "What you done, hired a drifter you think is on the dodge?"

"I tried to, but he wouldn't hire," Leona reported.

Lambert followed her outside. He said hesitantly, "It's none of my business, Miss Leona, but I dislike to see you start a ruckus with Tate Usher. Bar Bell won't win nothin' in a fight against TU. It'd be better to meet Tate halfway, and settle things peaceable."

"That's what my father did," Leona scoffed. "And so has everyone else. We've met Usher halfway so many times his TU steers are crowding us out of business."

"Every move Tate made was legal," Lambert argued. "You can't blame a man for bein' ambitious. Cowmen been tryin' to get more grass and water ever since the Israelites ran their cattle on the mesas east of Jerusalem. It's a real old-timey habit that nothin' ever changes."

"It's high time someone tried changing it then," Leona declared. "I'm going to try, along with Ben Petty who has decided to join me. And there'll be others."

"Petty!" Lambert snorted. "Why, your own foreman claims Petty has been eatin' Bar Bell beef for years!"

Leona shrugged. She said cynically, "I'd welcome the devil himself, if he knew how to shoot a gun."

She went on to Morgan's Mercantile then, and Sheriff Lambert muttered, "She's got a go-to-hell streak in her, by grab. She has for a fact!"

Ten minutes later Clark Morgan expressed approximately the same opinion. He sat at his desk on the rear balcony of the Mercantile, a fashionably garbed, pursy-mouthed man who had built up a profitable banking and freighting business after inheriting this store from his father. "You've got a rebel's temper," he said censuringly. "It may cost you Bar Bell one of these days."

Leona left her chair and moved around the

12

desk, and when Morgan rose with habitual courtesy, she noticed how his narrow shoulders exag-
gerated a slightly bulging midriff. In a land of
tanned, slim-hipped horsemen, he seemed pudgy
and pale; yet — and she consciously tallied this in
his favor — Clark Morgan could buy and sell
most of the men in Bunchgrass Basin. . . .

"So now I'm a rebel," she murmured with
mock concern. She made an open-palmed gesture with her hands and insisted, "I've got no
choice, Clark. There's upward of three hundred
TU steers on Tonto Flats right now, with more
drifting through the Tailholts every day. I need
that graze for winter feed, and there's only one
way to save it."

"But you have neither the men nor the money
for a fight against TU," Morgan objected.

Leona eyed him with frank speculation, remembering that this modest merchant had once
asked her to marry him. It had been an almost
formal proposal, without passion or eagerness.
Yet he'd seemed genuinely disappointed when
she refused him.

"I can hire the men," she said, "if you'll lend
me the money."

Morgan frowned. He asked, "Do you realize
what you'd be up against, Lee? A range war is a
messy business. Perhaps you think Tate Usher is
bluffing, and perhaps he is. But once the
shooting starts it won't be just Usher you'll be
dealing with. It'll be men like Idaho Cleek, and
Lee Pardee and Red Naviska."

"With a good-sized loan I could hire men like them," Leona said stubbornly.

"It would be a foolish transaction for both of us," Morgan counseled. "Bar Bell was in poor shape when your father died. It's no better off now. The thing for you to do is to sit tight and wait."

"Wait for what?" Leona demanded.

A secretive smile eased Morgan's lips. He said, "I happen to know that Usher strained his credit when he brought in that big bunch of Mexican-run steers. He gambled on a rise in beef prices which didn't materialize. Now he's dickering with the Indian Agency to make contract delivery the first of the year."

"By that time my winter graze would be gone," Leona said. "I've got to save it now, while there's something to save."

Morgan sighed. "I don't see how it can be accomplished, Lee. Honestly I don't."

"Then you won't lend me the money?"

Morgan shook his head. "Running a ranch is no job for a woman, much less running a range war. Why don't you sell out at a fair price and move into town?"

"Never!" Leona exclaimed.

She picked up her gloves and stood for a moment, angrily whipping them against the palm of her left hand. "I'll never let Bar Bell go, no matter what happens!"

Then she asked, "Would you also refuse to lend your wife money, if you had a wife?"

14

Morgan reached out and patted her arm with a tallow-white hand. He said, "My wife would automatically own half of what I possess. She could spend it as she chose." His fingers tightened on her arm and a warmth came into his eyes. He said sternly, "But she would live with me, here in town."

"Why, Clark," Leona said, and laughed at him.

She crossed the balcony, eyeing him over her shoulder and smiling back at him. Just before she started down the rear stairway she said, "A wife usually lives with her husband, Clark."

Whereupon she went downstairs and narrowly avoided colliding with Tate Usher in the doorway. The big, bland-faced rancher stepped aside and bowed and said, "Beg pardon." He chuckled as if enjoying some secret joke and asked, "How's your foreman, Miss Leona — still bedfast?"

"Yes," she said curtly, "which is why your Mex steers haven't been run off Tonto Flats."

"My, my," Usher said, the words merging into sly laughter.

Leona went on out to the street and presently, as she passed the courthouse on her way to Doc Medwick's home, she noticed that Idaho Cleek was sitting on the jail stoop conversing with Sheriff Lambert. That, added to Morgan's refusal to grant a loan, increased the sense of frustration which the stranger had spawned at Commissary Creek.

"Damn them," she whispered. "Damn them all!"

15

2. As a Man Remembers

Jeff Tennant halted his horse on a bluff at the northern edge of Tonto Flats and contemplated the familiar run of country ahead of him. The lower hills looked exactly as he remembered them — like dusty elephants asleep in the sun. Above them the timbered slopes rose in rough-and-tumble disorder, and beyond, veiled in autumn haze, was the high wall of Dragoon Divide.

All the contours of this land suited Tennant, and pleased him, in the way a man is pleased by the build of a race horse, or a well-made woman; and because he knew every nook and cranny of the Tailholts, Tennant saw more than his eyes beheld: grassy, tree-bordered meadows and bald benches and long, shaded corridors in the pines. But clearer than any of these was the picture of his homestead cabin with a Roman Four burned on its door.

"Wonder if it's still there," Tennant mused. "Pine logs burn easy."

A tolerable amount of toil had gone into the building of that cabin; tedious, painstaking toil which had turned hand-hewed logs and timbers into the best-constructed home in the Tailholt Hills. He had hauled adobe dirt all the way from Spanish Canyon, had mixed it with straw and tromped it into chinking mud with his bare feet. He had built a stout, tight cabin, and Jane

16

Medwick had called it his "Shack of Dreams."

The need for revenge was like a malignant growth inside Jeff Tennant; it had shaped all his thoughts for three hellish years in Yuma Prison. But now the idea of eating supper at his own table and sleeping under his own roof whetted a new eagerness in him. He thought, *I can be home before dark — if I've still got a home.*

The pictures in his mind kept Tennant company as he rode, and some of them were like laughing companions. There was the picture of a poker game the night he'd won twelve hundred dollars from Big Sid Stromberg. He'd had less than twenty dollars in his pocket when he went into the Palace Saloon and Stromberg invited him to try his luck at head-to-head stud. Old Dame Fortune had been with him all the way that night; he'd won the first five pots, and after that there'd been no stopping him. Next morning he had paid off a thousand-dollar-loan note with interest at Morgan's Mercantile. . . .

Then there was the picture of Jane Medwick, a tall and supple girl whose eyes were the blue-gray color of campfire smoke. He had endeavored to discard that picture at Yuma, many times; but it was with him now, making him remember the slow sweetness of her smile, the yielding cushion of her lips — the way she closed her eyes when he kissed her.

Thus, for a time, Jeff Tennant's thoughts ran full and free and he was glad to be riding home with the good smell of dust and leather and horse sweat in his nostrils. But when he came close to the hills, Tennant scanned the cattle he passed with mounting wonderment. This had always been Bar Bell range, yet most of the cow brutes he saw were slat-ribbed Sonora steers wearing Tate Usher's TU above a vented "bug" brand.

"So that's it," he reflected. "That's why Leona Bell is looking for a tough ramrod."

Recalling that her pompous, peace-loving father had been a member of the jury which convicted him of brand-blotting three years ago, Tennant took a cynical satisfaction in the knowledge that Usher was now crowding Bar Bell. . . .

The trail dipped occasionally, crossing dry washes and winding through rock-studded canyons, but always it gained altitude and by mid-afternoon Tennant rode into a stand of high-branched timber. Pine needles muffled the tromp of his horse here, and the rarefied air carried the fine odors of pitch and pine and moist, tree-shaded earth. When he crossed a grassy meadow Tennant counted upward of twenty grazing steers, over half of which wore TU brands. He tallied five Lazy P's, belonging to Ben Petty whose bachelor camp was beyond the next ridge, and presently passed an old brindle cow with a brindle calf, both bearing his Roman Four brand.

Pennant thought instantly, *Someone's been good enough to rep for me!*

The knowledge both pleased and surprised him, for he had expected that his calves would go

18

unbranded and thus become mavericks — fair game for any man with a rope and running iron.

Later, as Tennant topped the ridge above Petty's place, the sound of gunfire drifted up to him. He quickly crossed the crest and, halting on the north rim, listened to another burst of shooting. Six reports in rapid succession. He waited out an interval of silence; when the gun blasts came again he reckoned their origin as being near the base of this ridge, and counting six shots, said, "Sounds like target practice."

Whereupon he rode down the slope and soon glimpsed Ben Petty walking away from a flour-sack target tied to a tree. The lanky homesteader stepped off ten paces, whirled and fired at the target. Then he peered at the untouched circle in the flour sack and cursed dejectedly.

"Practice makes perfect," Tennant called, announcing his presence.

Petty flinched. His homely, high-beaked face reddened and he said, "So they finally turned you loose." He came over to the trail, not offering to shake hands, and added, "All the danged practice in the world wouldn't make me perfect."

"Takes time," Tennant said. He drew his gun and snapped two shots at the flour sack, and when Petty stared at the twin holes near the circle's center, Tennant explained. "I couldn't do that a couple months ago, Ben. I've practiced every day since I got out of jail."

Petty eyed him sharply. "So you're planning to

kill Tate Usher," he said, in the slow way of a man thinking aloud.

"At the right time, and in the right place," Tennant said.

"But how about Idaho Cleek?" Petty asked. "He's always close by his boss. How you goin' to fight Usher without fightin' Cleek too?"

Tennant shrugged, having found no answer to that problem himself. Presently he said, "Saw a fresh-branded brindle calf back yonder. Who's been repping for Roman Four?"

"Me," Petty muttered. He put his rope-calloused fingers to building a cigarette and added, "Might of missed more'n' I branded."

The thought came to Tennant that Ben hadn't changed. He had never offered more than a grudging civility, which was all he offered now. But he had taken the trouble to brand Roman Four calves, and so Tennant said, "I'm much obliged to you, Ben, and I'll return the favor, first chance I get."

Then he asked, "What happened to Claude Bell?"

"Died," Petty reported. "Guess he worried hisself to death. Two dry years burned up the graze. Commissary Creek shrunk to a trickle and things got awful tough. When it finally came up a few rains Tate Usher imported a big herd of Mexican steers and crowded the whole damn range. There's TU stuff strung out all the way from Tonto flats to the Rio Pago, and them starved steers is gobblin' three bites to every one our critters take. They'll have it ate down smooth as the palm of a tinhorn's hand in another couple months. Then we'll have two choices — we can sell out to Usher at his price, or borrow money to buy feed and go busted. Either way we lose and Usher wins."

Then he asked, "You remember what a nice outfit Joe Barlow had?"

Tennant nodded.

"Well, Joe quit the cow business. He sold out to Usher and bought the Senate Hotel in Quadrille. Now his wife works in the kitchen, Rose waits on table, young Billy is swamper and Joe drinks up the profits at Big Sid Stromberg's saloon."

"A hell of a way to make a living," Tennant muttered, and remembered that Petty had been Rose Barlow's bashful admirer three years ago. "Why did Joe sell out?"

"On account of what happened to Mac Menafee, I guess. You knew Mac was on Usher's pay roll, didn't you? Well, he was supposed to homestead that section betwixt the Pot Holes and Bandoleer Breaks for Usher. But he got hisself married and when the time came to turn the place over to TU, Mac decided he wanted to keep it — his wife having a baby on the way, and all. He borrowed money to pay Usher back the wages he'd drawed whilst he was proving up on the section, but Usher wouldn't take it. He said a deal was a deal. Six months later Idaho Cleek crowded Menafee into a fight on Main Street and killed him deader'n hell. Mac's widow went back to Texas and when the county put the place up at tax sale, Usher bid it in. Joe Barlow saw Cleek kill Menafee. He told me Mac had his gun half raised before Cleek made his grab. He said Cleek's draw was faster'n the flick of a toad's tongue. I guess Joe was thinking about that when he sold his ranch."

"Shouldn't wonder," Tennant said, and recalling how Jules Huffmeyer had once expressed the opinion that Idaho Cleek wasn't as tough as he talked, asked, "Is Huffmeyer still straw boss at Bar Bell?"

"Yeah, but a bronc fell on him a month ago and Jules ain't doin' so good. Leona stopped by today. Said she was going after Doc Medwick because Jules' busted ribs ain't mendin' like they should."

Tennant thought. *No wonder she's looking for a ramrod.* He was riding away when Petty said, "Usher is using your place as a line camp now. Ed Peebles is there, and I hope you have to blast him out with a bullet in the belly."

Ben took off his hat, revealing a bandage where the hair had been shaved from his scalp. "The drunken son got fresh with Rose Saturday night. When I took a poke at him he pistol-whipped me. That's why I'm learnin' how to shoot straight. I'm goin' to fight Peebles with his own tools one of these days."

"Maybe you won't have to," Tennant suggested. "Maybe I'll kick him off my place so hard there won't be anything left for you to shoot at."

Doctor Medwick sat relaxed on the well-padded seat of his red-wheeled buggy and allowed his bay pacer to shuffle slowly up the road. This was five miles north of Commissary Creek, near the fork which led to Bar Bell. Doc lit up his second cigar since supper, feeling a trifle guilty and recalling an old scene out of the past — a time long ago when Jane's mother was alive and when a dollar was hard to come by. He'd been strictly rationed to one cigar a day, but occasionally, when a customer paid a bill or some other unexpected good fortune befell them, he had celebrated with a second cigar, whereupon six-year-old Jane would exclaim censuringly, "Look Mommy — two at a day!"

Doc chuckled, remembering all the fun they'd had in those days when Quadrille was a hurly-burly mining camp and cowtown combined. He'd brought his bride to the Senate Hotel, intending to lavish the luxury of hotel living on her indefinitely. But within one week's time she had prodded him into starting construction on a home of their own, choosing a site near the Big Arroyo bridge: "So I can hear you coming home when you've been to some ranch late at night."

A long time ago. Now Jane was as her mother had been. She looked the same and cooked the same, and was ready for marriage. But Jane was waiting for a man who might never return, and who might be unworthy of her if he came back. Doc was thinking about that when he heard horses behind him; turning, he saw Tate Usher and Idaho Cleek come jogging along the road.

They drew abreast of the rig, Usher saying good-naturedly, "Nice night for a drive, eh, Doc?"

"Fine evening," Medwick agreed, and glanced at Cleek. The hatchet-faced foreman barely nodded; he had a secretive, sardonic way with him which was in direct contrast to Usher's loud, loose-tongued talk.

"Going to Bar Bell?" Usher inquired, keeping his horse alongside the rig.

Medwick nodded, whereupon Usher said amusedly, "Better not cure Huffmeyer too soon, Doc. Leona says them broken ribs is the only thing that keeps Bar Bell from starting a ruckus with TU. And she told Sheriff Lambert she was fixing for a fight."

He laughed, adding slyly, "That would be odd — her fighting me."

They rode on ahead then and Doc muttered to himself, "Not half as odd as you fighting her."

Watching them fade into the dust-hazed twilight, Medwick noticed how ill-matched a pair they made, with Usher's flabby bulk accentuating the reed-thin shape of his foreman. They were as unlike as two men could be, yet they seemed to work in perfect harmony and were seldom separated.

When Medwick turned into the Bar Bell road

he got to thinking about the night Leona's mother died. Tate Usher had come for him at suppertime, and on the way to TU had explained how Mrs. Bell had been thrown as she was mounting a spirited horse that was unaccustomed to side saddle and women's riding skirts. Tate hadn't bothered to explain why Claude Bell's wife was visiting at TU, which was then a ramshackle, one-man outfit. But Doc had guessed that the reason was partly due to the fact that Bell was twice the age of his pretty, vivacious wife and partly due to Tate Usher's good looks. For Tate had been a heller with the women before prosperity and soft living turned him flabby fat.

Medwick bit off the soggy end of his cigar and spat it out. But he couldn't banish the distasteful memory of Mrs. Bell staring up at Usher and pleading, "Don't let our little girl know, Tate. Don't ever let her know."

Our little girl!

Now Leona Bell was threatening to fight Tate Usher, and Tate was saying how odd that would be. . . .

3. The Shack of Dreams

It was coming sundown when Tennant rode into his unfenced yard. Everything looked about the same as he'd left it three years ago. The cabin's pinewood logs had weathered a trifle; the Roman Four brand on the door didn't show quite as plain, and the corral gate sagged badly. *Hinges need resetting,* Tennant thought, and saw a roan bronc trot across the corral. Peebles' double-rigged saddle hung on the kak pole, yet no smoke came from the cabin's stovepipe and Tennant wondered why the TU rider wasn't cooking supper. And why the door was closed.

When the roan nickered a greeting Tennant kept a strict watch on the cabin's two front windows, his right hand close to holster. But there was no sign of life, and so he called, "Hello the house!"

Then he waited, entirely puzzled. Unless Peebles kept two horses and two saddles, he was here. A man wouldn't go far afoot. It occurred to Tennant that the TU puncher might be forted up in the cabin, waiting for a fight. . . .

"Hell with him," Tennant muttered, and keeping a wary watch, rode to the cabin.

Still no sign nor sound of movement. Tennant peered at a cobwebbed window, but the glass was too dirty to see through. He called, "Anybody home?" and waited another long moment

26

before dismounting. If trouble were coming, it should come now. He nudged his gun loose in its leather, stood at one side of the door and opened it.

Smoke billowed out with a wave of room-trapped odors the like of which Jeff Tennant had never smelled at one time: an acrid stench that was like a rubbish fire, a branding corral, and a Saturday night saloon combined. Presently, as the smoke thinned, he saw Ed Peebles sprawled on the smouldering tick of a brass bed.

The fire, which hadn't touched Peebles' slack-jawed face, had burned the tick down to the bed's sagging slats all along the front edge. It smouldered beneath Peebles' fully clad body, and the cardboard tag of a Durham sack in his shirt pocket was burning now. Tennant grabbed a bucket of water from the wash bench beside the door; he doused the tick and hurriedly toting another bucketful from the windmill water trough, doused the tick again for good measure.

Then Tennant considered the smoke-fogged, disordered room. On a shelf above the bed was a dust-covered copy of *Blackstone's Commentaries*, symbol of an old Texan's desire that his son should be a lawyer; and two tally books, one of which contained layout plans for the house, blacksmith shop, sheds and corrals Tennant had dreamed of building here. There was a quart whiskey bottle, less than half full, on a chair near the bed and two empty bottles on the dish-littered table.

Tennant thought, *Ed staged a spree, went to bed with a lighted cigarette, and when the tick caught fire, the smoke smothered him. . . .*

He felt no pity for the dead rider. But the stink of this smoke-fouled, filthy room sickened him. He went outside, watered his horse, filled his canteen and opened the corral gate so Peebles' bronc could shift for itself. Then he rode up the triple-toed slope south of his cabin, and making camp, had a frugal supper cooked at dusk.

Afterward, while the ruddy embers of his fire turned to ash, Tennant reviewed the monstrous fraud which had banished him from this country three years ago. He had driven his little bunch of steers to town slowly, wanting to retain every pound of tallow, and so it was almost dark when he choused them into a pen at the Quadrille stockyards. He'd taken Jane Medwick to a dance that night, celebrating an occasion which had seemed vastly more important than the money involved simply because it had taken two tedious years of effort. Because Jane had seemed sweeter than seven sticks of Christmas candy he had come within a horse hair of asking her to marry him. He'd sure felt big for his britches that night. But next morning, with a cattle buyer tallying the twenty steers and Sheriff Lambert acting as brand inspector, he'd felt lower than snake sign in a wheel rut when Lambert challenged three animals whose TU brands had been worked over into Roman Fours. . . .

"Crude," the old lawman had announced. "Tol'able crude."

And so they were. Three botched brands contrived by lengthening the tops of the T's so that they ran across the tops of the U's which were reburned to resemble V's; then another line burned across the bottom to form the base of a Roman Four, Tennant knew he would have noticed them yesterday if the steers had been in the bunch he'd driven to town; yet the altered brands were old enough to be well scabbed. Almost at once he'd guessed the answer — had known beyond shadow of doubt that Tate Usher had rigged this deal beforehand and framed him during the night. But there'd been no telltale tracks to prove that the TU steers had been substituted for three of his own. All he'd found was a couple of boot prints in the deep dust at one side of the pen gate, and they didn't match, one being a full inch shorter than the other.

Tennant remembered now that Sheriff Lambert had seemed sorry to arrest him; that old Doc Medwick had offered to import a lawyer from Tucson, and that Jane had brought a chocolate cake to the courthouse jail. But because they'd all believed him guilty he had told them all to go to hell. . . .

The hoof pound of a running horse interrupted Tennant's sober reflections. Quickly stomping out the last remnants of his campfire he listened as a horse crossed the ridge, heading south. When the remote rumor of travel finally

29

faded he thought, *Someone heading for Ben's place,* and wondered who could be visiting Petty at this time of night.

He was thinking about that when he pulled off his boots. It occurred to him that the rider might have stopped by the cabin, in which case he was probably taking word of Peeble's death to Ben, and to Sheriff Lambert.

"Ben can quit his target practice now," Tennant reflected, and presently went to sleep.

Some time later he awoke to find himself sitting up, gun in hand. For a moment he didn't know what had aroused him, and mistaking moonrise for daybreak, thought he'd had his sleep out. Then a fast-traveling horse passed so close he heard its gusty, labored breathing. Tennant hurried around a windfall that barred his view; he saw a horse and rider go down the north slope, disappearing into the lower shadows where moonlight hadn't reached.

The hoofbeats died out and Tennant went back to his blanket, stepping now with barefooted caution. He thought, *One rode south and another rode north and they were in a hell of a hurry.* It occurred to him that both trips might have been made by the same rider. But why? Whether one man or two, why all this nighthawking?

Shrugging off the riddle of that, Tennant shaped up a cigarette and smoked it. This country was full of riddles, none of which greatly concerned him. Or so he thought. His plans were simple, and complete. Tomorrow he would ride to Quadrille and wait for a chance to force Tate Usher into drawing a gun against him. It might take a little time, and a bit of maneuvering, for Usher was no bragging bully given to casual violence. The showdown would have to occur in town, so there'd be reliable witnesses. And it had to be at a time when Idaho Cleek wasn't beside his boss. For even though Tennant considered himself a better than average gunhand, he had no illusions about his skill as compared with Cleek's. The TU foreman was a wizard with a gun. . . .

As if in echo to that thought, the sound of shooting drifted up to Tennant — three spaced blasts that ran raggedly back through the hills. Tennant discarded his cigarette, taking care to toss it into the campfire's ashes. He put on his socks and boots, listening for further sound and hearing none. But presently, as he saddled his horse, the smell of wood smoke came faintly to him; when he rode out to the rim of the ridge he saw a flare of flames above his cabin.

"The dirty sons!" he said savagely. "The dirty, stinking sons!"

Ben Petty was pouring his breakfast coffee when Tennant rode into the Lazy P yard. Ben came to the door, shading his sleep-swollen eyes against morning's first sunlight; he said glumly, "Come on in," and filled another cup.

Tennant seated himself at the table and blew steam from his coffee. "You have a visitor last night?" he inquired.

Petty shook his head.

"Well," Tennant reported, "somebody rode from my cabin to your corral, and back again."

This news didn't interest Ben at all. He went on with his eating for a full moment before he asked, "Why would anyone rim around here in the dark?"

"That depends," Tennant said. He reached for a hot biscuit before asking, "Did you tell folks in town that you were gunning for Peebles?"

Petty nodded. "Told everybody within earshot, whilst Doc Medwick was bandaging my head."

"So that's it," Tennant mused.

"That's what?" Petty asked irritably.

"It explains the things I saw at first daylight this morning," Tennant said. "Except for me being camped on Trinity Ridge last night, you'd be good as in Yuma Prison right now, Ben — or dangling from a scaffold."

Ben Petty gulped and put down his coffee cup. All the drowsiness went out of his eyes and he demanded, "What the hell you talkin' about?"

Tennant told him of finding Peebles dead, of seeing a rider cross the ridge, and hearing shots. "I couldn't figure it out, until I saw my cabin on fire. Then I guessed it had something to do with you. At daylight I took a close look at what was left of Ed Peebles. Somebody put a slug through his head, and probably a couple more through his back. Then they doused the shack with coal oil and set fire to it, figuring a coroner would discover where bullets had busted through bone, and that Ed's body would be too badly burned to show that he'd been dead before the shots were fired."

For a long moment Ben Petty sat in shocked silence. Finally he said, "And those tracks from your cabin to here would make it look like I done it."

Tennant nodded. "It's my guess that Tate Usher and Idaho Cleek must've stopped by to see Ed on their way home from town. When they found him dead of suffocation they saw a good chance of framing you off your place — like they framed me off mine."

Afterward he added thoughtfully, "I saw something else at Roman Four. Something that might prove Usher was present at that other frame-up three years ago."

Ben Petty poured himself another cup of coffee. "I guess a jury would of convicted me on circumstantial evidence," he said. "I'd be a gone goose sure enough, except for you."

"It makes an airtight case," Tennant agreed. "You publicly threatened to kill Peebles. He's found dead, and there's a set of tracks running from your place to Roman Four, and back again."

Then he said, "I'm an ex-convict, Ben. A jury might not accept my testimony about finding Peebles dead from suffocation."

The impact of that showed in Petty's eyes. And in his voice when he exclaimed, "But it's the truth! They got to believe the truth, no matter who tells it!"

A cynical smile eased Tennant's lips. He regarded Ben scornfully and asked, "Did they believe me three years ago? Did you?"

Ben slowly shook his head. . . .

"The truth is too damn simple," Tennant scoffed. "Folks want something fancy, and complicated; something a smart lawyer can build up with words, like a painted picture."

Ben asked, "You studied to be a lawyer for a spell, didn't you?"

"One year," Tennant said. "Then I decided I'd rather associate with horses."

"You figger I'd have a chance in court, if they didn't believe your story?"

Tennant shook his head.

"It'd be murder," Petty muttered. "The charge would be murder."

He got up and walked across the room and took his gun gear from a peg beside the door. "They ain't goin' to railroad me, like they did you," he said nervously. "By God, I'll leave the country first."

"Which is exactly what Usher wants you to do," Tennant reminded him. "Tate Usher doesn't give a damn where you go, just so you leave. He wants this range — all of it."

Ben strapped on his gun belt, his fingers fumbling the buckle. It wasn't overly warm in the shack but now perspiration greased his frowning face and he kept glancing furtively at the front window, canting his head to listen. "I'm goin' to hide out in the hills for a spell," he muttered. "I'm goin' to wait and see if Sheriff Sam believes your story. You reckon he will?"

"No telling about that," Tennant said. "But there's one way we might make it stand up. If we could get Doc Medwick to Roman Four ahead of anyone else there might be a good chance to prove what really happened."

"Then what in hell you waitin' on?" Petty demanded. "Why ain't you hightailin' for town to get Doc?"

"Because I don't believe he's home," Tennant said, smiling a little at the swift change in Petty. A few moments ago he'd been sleepy and dull-eyed, interested only in eating breakfast. Now he was eager and impatient; he was like a tight-strung wire, twanging at the slightest contact. "You said Leona went to get Doc yesterday. Well, I started for town this morning and saw one set of wheel tracks in the road. Medwick must've driven to Bar Bell last night and stayed over."

"Then I'll go fetch him right now," Ben declared. "I'll tell him the whole story, just like you told me."

"No," Tennant objected. "Not the whole story. Just tell Doc the part about me finding Peebles smothered. Also one thing more, Ben, and this is important. There's a set of boot prints in the mud near the watering trough. Tell Doc I

35

want him to measure them exactly, and copy the outlines. Tell him to be sure he gets those measurements correct to the fraction of an inch."

"Won't you be at Roman Four when Doc gets there?" Petty demanded.

Tennant shook his head. "I'm going to Quadrille to make my report to Lambert. I'll tell him I found Peebles smothered, and save the rest of my story until it's needed."

Petty looked worried again. "How about them boot prints?" he asked. "Supposin' they was made by the same size boots I wear?"

"What size you wear?" Tennant inquired casually.

"Eight and a half."

"On both feet?"

"Of course," Petty said.

"Then both those prints won't be the same as yours," Tennant told him.

"But who ever saw a man wear different size boots?" Petty demanded.

"I have," Tennant said, "and I'll be seeing him again — real soon, I hope."

"What's his name?"

"That," Tennant admitted, "is what I've got to find out."

Petty eyed him wonderingly. "It sounds loco as a drunkard's dream," he complained. "But mebbe you know what you're doing."

Then he hurried out to the horse corral.

At about this same time, Idaho Cleek stood in

36

the office doorway at TU's headquarters on the Rio Pago, giving out the day's riding orders to five men assembled before him. His three gold teeth glinted in the early sunshine, bright mementos of a fist fight ten years ago. He had lost three front teeth in that fight and had never lifted a hand against a man since, unless that hand held a gun. . . .

"You," Cleek said, indicating young Johnny Peebles, "ride up and help your brother push the rest of them Sonora steers down to Tonto Flats. There's upward of two hundred head between Menafee Camp and the Bar Bell road."

Johnny, whose cheeks still held a boyish fuzz in lieu of beard, asked hopefully, "You want I should stay with Ed until the job is done?"

"Yes," Cleek said, his milky-blue eyes showing no change, "and keep away from Ben Petty's place. That damn maverick hates Ed's guts."

Lee Pardee chuckled. "Rose Barlow sure struck Ed's fancy," he reflected with a sly wink at the others.

And Red Naviska said, "She's liable to make a Gentle Annie out of Ed — a regular Romeo."

"Romeo hell!" Johnny blurted, bristling like a ruffled pup. "Ed ain't —"

"Go on, go on," Cleek ordered gruffly. "This ain't no time for funnin'. There's work to do."

4. "God A'mighty!"

Jeff Tennant reached Quadrille shortly before noon, the tromp of his horse setting up a bonging sound as he crossed the plank bridge at the west end of town. Remembering how difficult a time he'd had chousing his twenty steers across here three years ago, Tennant grinned reflectively. He'd cussed them in the dust-hazed twilight, never guessing that he had an audience; he'd called their mothers heifer harlots and their sire a white-faced hellion of uncertain ancestry; when he finally got them all across the bridge there was Jane Medwick standing at her front gate, inviting him to supper. . . .

And now, as Tennant glanced at Doc Medwick's little white house, he loosed a gusty grunt of pleasure. For he was seeing Jane come quickly down the veranda steps; was hearing her exclaim, "Jeff — Jeff Tennant!"

The thought came to him that this was exactly as he'd pictured it: Jane running to meet him with a glow in her eyes and a smile making twin dimples in her cheeks. He dismounted and took her hand and there was a moment when the impulse to take her in his arms was like the tantalizing itch of a half-healed wound. But he resisted the impulse; he rocked back on his heels, regarding her soberly and saying, "The man hadn't seen the girl for a long time, so he looked

38

at her real close, not meaning any harm."

This was an old game they'd played the first time he'd taken her to a dance, using it as a mutual bridge between strangers, and so now she asked with mock concern, "What did the man think of the girl?"

"Well," Tennant said, eyeing her critically from face to feet and back again, "he saw very little change. Hair still the same off-shade sorrel, eyes the color of wood smoke on a windless morning, face a bit on the thin side, except when she smiles — to show off her dimples."

Then he grinned and announced heartily, "No improvement at all. Just the prettiest girl east or west of the Pecos!"

"The man still has his blarney ways with women," Jane said, frankly pleased. "He knows how to get himself invited to supper." She retrieved her hand, eyed the slim fingers he had squeezed, and said, "If they aren't broken I'll bake you a chocolate cake."

"Chocolate cake!" Tennant exclaimed, and smacked his lips. "I knew there was some reason I'd ought to pay you a visit, but I'd forgotten there was such a thing as chocolate cake."

"That's one thing you and Dad agree on," Jane said smilingly. She glanced down the road, adding, "Dad went to Bar Bell last night and should be home any time. I've been watching for him."

"He'll be a trifle late," Tennant reported. "Ed Peebles went on a one-man spree, set fire to my shack and smothered to death. I sent word to Doc."

"How horrible!" Jane exclaimed.

"I don't care about his dying," Tennant said, "but I wish he'd picked some other place to do it in."

"The Shack of Dreams," Jane murmured. She plucked at his sleeve and said softly, "You can make all those fine dreams come true, Jeff."

"Still got faith in your favorite brand-blotter?" Tennant asked self-mockingly.

Jane's smile faded, taking the dimples with it. She said, "I never really believed that, Jeff. You took it for granted."

She met his eyes fully, as if willing to have him see all there was to see, and to know how it was with her. "Didn't you get my letter?" she asked.

Tennant nodded, ashamed now that his overwhelming resentment had included this loyal, warm-eyed girl. "I never was good at writing letters in jail," he said.

"It must've been awful," Jane said, and studied his face as if reckoning what damage the prison years had done. "Dad tried to get you pardoned, Jeff. But nothing ever came of it."

For a long moment then they stood in silence, having no easy way of telling the things that needed to be told. Finally Tennant said, "I'm going to notify Lambert about Peebles. Then I'll get a shearing at Biddle's barbershop and be back in time for supper."

He stepped into saddle, and Jane said, almost

40

pleadingly, "Don't do anything foolish, Jeff."

It was, he understood, her way of asking him to forget the past; to forget what Sheriff Lambert and those other damned fools had done to him. He smiled down at her, not knowing the smile didn't reach his eyes, and said, "Nothing foolish."

Then he gave her a comradely salute and rode on along Main Street. Jane, he guessed, was wondering what he intended to do about Tate Usher. And everyone else in this town would be wondering the same thing. Especially Sheriff Lambert. The mealy-mouthed old lawdog would probably try to talk him out of doing anything, which was a specialty with Lambert. He'd made a career of doing nothing; in a country gripped by one man's greed, Sheriff Lambert preached a policy of peace at any price.

To hell with him, Tennant thought. He passed Swanson's Feed Store, and turning in at McGonigle's Livery, peered down at the ape-featured Irishman in the doorway. "A mean-looking Mick if ever I saw one," he proclaimed solemnly.

"Jeff — ye spalpeen!" Tay McGonigle blurted. " 'Tis glad I am to see ye back bejasus!"

Afterward, while McGonigle led his horse down the long runway to a rear stall, Tennant gave Main Street a leisurely appraisal. Quadrille, he reflected, hadn't changed at all. The same old adobe and false-fronted frame buildings lined both sides of this street, and half of them were

41

vacant — disintegrating reminders of a long-gone era when Quadrille had been the toughest town between Lordsburg and Tucson. There was the old Bonanza Bazaar, where Lillie Langtry's golden voice had roused rafter-shaking applause; the Gilded Cage Dancehall with its cobwebbed windows and sagging gallery; the Silver Stud Saloon, the Belladonna, the Rosebud and Ace High — roofless, weather-warped monuments to free-spending miners who'd once swarmed the Calico Queen diggings five miles east of Quadrille.

North of Main Street and running parallel with it was Fremont Street where the merchants of this town had their comfortable homes. One long block south of Main, perched along the bank of Big Arroyo, was Sashay Alley which ran crookedly east to the stockyards. Here were the crumbling, blanket-windowed huts, the countless barking dogs and pungent odors of Old Mexico. Here also was the parlor house of Mayme Shay, handy by the stockyards where trail crews camped.

Tennant sauntered along the plank walk and thought, *It even smells the same.* There was the horsy reek of McGonigle's stable, the acrid taint of Phil Burleson's blacksmith forge, and presently, as he passed Morgan's Mercantile, the tangy, aromatic mixture of fresh-ground coffee and vinegar and coal oil. But because three years in Yuma Prison had changed him, the town didn't *feel* the same.

Clark Morgan stepped from the Post Office doorway, peered at Tennant, and said civilly, "Hello. Going back to your homestead, I presume."

Tennant nodded, seeing no change in Morgan. The merchant-banker, he guessed, wasn't more than thirty-five years old, yet he had the precise and dignified ways of an old man. "I might be in to see you about a loan later on," Tennant said. "Reckon you can spare the cash?"

"No," Morgan said promptly.

Tennant waited for an explanation, and when none was offered he said, "I've been told your father made a fortune by using that word at the right time."

If Morgan resented this sarcasm he showed no sign of it. "Refusing to make loans is a banker's privilege," he said and walked away.

Tennant shrugged. He thought, *No credit for ex-convicts.* That meant he'd have to take time to gather a little jag of steers and sell them before he could build a cabin. . . .

Mayme Shay came out of the Bon Ton Millinery, a tall, broad-bosomed woman whose fashionable clothes and breezy good humor had become a Quadrille tradition, along with her parlor house. She smiled at Tennant, and when he tipped his hat, she stopped beside him and said, "I saw Clark Morgan walk off like he was afraid you'd pick his pockets. You need a grubstake, Jeff?"

Tennant shook his head, grinned, and said,

"Thanks just the same." Then he asked, "Did Hobo Bill locate that Spanish treasure chest while I've been gone?"

"Not unless he's keeping it a secret," Mayme said, and her lusty laughter was good to hear. "Sometimes I think Bill doesn't care whether he finds it or not. It's the looking that he likes. Gives him something to dream about."

Tennant was considering that as he walked toward the courthouse. *Something to dream about.* He'd had dreams aplenty before he went to Yuma. He looked into Lambert's office and found it deserted; whereupon he quartered across the street to the Palace Saloon.

Big Sid Stromberg stood behind the bar, absently polishing its rosewood surface while Joe Barlow downed his first drink of the day. Stromberg nodded a wordless greeting, his chalky face showing neither surprise nor pleasure.

Joe Barlow swung around at once and exclaimed, "They said you'd never come back, Jeff, but I knowed damned well you would!"

He came to meet Tennant, walking in the strict fashion of a man seldom sober; he shook hands limply and eyed Tennant's face as if searching for some important sign, and asked, "You've come to stay, ain't you, Jeff? You ain't just ridin' through?"

Tennant grinned. "I'm staying," he said. He looked into Barlow's watery, wavering eyes and felt a quick sense of pity for this wilted old cowman. Joe had never been a very big man, nor a very bold one, but he'd had his pride and his plans for the future. Now he had neither.

"Have a drink," Tennant invited.

"Don't mind if I do," Barlow said in a casual, disinterested way. But Tennant noticed that Joe licked his lips like a man burning with fever and that when Joe raised his glass some of the whiskey spilled.

Sid Stromberg dropped Tennant's silver dollar into the till and placed change on the bar. He glanced at the doorway as if expecting visitors. Then he said flatly, "I get considerable trade from the TU crew, and I dislike trouble in my place."

"So?" Tennant mused, remembering that Big Sid had served on the jury, and guessing that the saloonman had welcomed an opportunity of venting his spite. "That wouldn't be a left-handed way of saying I'm not welcome at your bar, would it, Sid?"

Stromberg took a cigar from his vest pocket. He bit off its end, then changed his mind and put the cigar back in the same pocket. "You heard what I said," he muttered crankily. He walked down to the end of the bar and picked up a copy of the Tombstone *Epitaph*.

"Don't mind Sid," Joe Barlow urged. "He ain't got no sense of humor."

"Maybe he needs a drink," Tennant reflected, a tough grin slanting his cheeks. "Or maybe he needs a punch on the nose."

That suggestion seemed to startle Joe Barlow. But it had no visible effect on Stromberg. The big saloonman continued his reading for a full moment before he said, "Any time you think you're man enough, just step up and say so."

This, Tennant realized, was a foolish thing to do. Stromberg outweighed him by thirty pounds or more and had a reputation for rough-and-tumble fighting. It was the sort of thing Jane had asked him not to do. But Tennant's rebellious streak had always been stronger than his caution, and it was now. He unbuckled his gun belt, handed the gear to Barlow, and announced, "I'm man enough, Stromberg."

Big Sid put down the paper. He took three cigars from his vest pocket and laid them on the bar. Then he sauntered out into the room, rubbing the knuckles of his right hand with his left palm and smiling in a thoroughly satisfied way. "Let's see if your fighting is any better than your brand-blotting," he taunted.

He was still smiling when Tennant pitched forward and hit him in the face.

The impact of knuckles against Stromberg's nose made a meaty sound above the scuff of Tennant's boots and it was echoed by a snarled curse as Big Sid dodged sideways, narrowly evading Tennant's second swing. Stromberg wheeled around; he shook his head, and blood's redness appeared below his flattened nostrils. But Tennant thought instantly, *He's not really hurt,* and knew how poor his chances were now.

He had gambled on gaining a quick advantage by hitting Stromberg hard enough to put him on the defensive; instead he had merely stung the saloonman into swift and savage action. . . .

"I'll stomp your guts into the floor!" Big Sid bellowed, and came at Tennant in the fist-cocked fashion of an accomplished slugger.

Tennant stood toe to toe with him, throwing punches and taking them against his guarding arms, until Stromberg broke this up with a sudden shift that appeared to be retreat. Tennant charged forward. He took a glancing blow that scraped a raw track high on his left cheek; he hit Stromberg in the belly with an upper-cutting right that made the big man squall a curse. Tennant grinned, and tried to target Sid's rage-rutted face. But Stromberg blocked the blow; he caught Tennant a trifle off balance and battered him with both fists. Tennant tripped over a chair — fell to his hands and knees. Stromberg leaned forward and aimed a long-looping right to Tennant's head. Tennant ducked, and was on his way up when Stromberg kicked him, the boot striking Tennant's shoulder hard enough to turn him completely around. Stromberg laughed, and tried another kick, and missed as Tennant jumped clear.

"Stand still and fight," Big Sid growled. He lunged into a slugging attack that forced Tennant steadily back.

The upper muscles of Tennant's right arm were completely numb now; he tried to circle, wanting time for the shock to wear off, but Stromberg kept boring in, kept forcing Tennant back until he was trapped between the bar's elbow and a front window, with the wall behind him.

Tennant slashed with his left, and hit Stromberg's nose again. He heard Sid snarl a curse, and saw the red smear his knuckles made as they glanced along Stromberg's cheek. He swung, and missed, and took a blow in the chest that staggered him. He was remotely aware of people at the window — glimpsed young Billy Barlow's tense, wide-eyed face pressed against the glass. He dodged a looping left and saw that fist smash into the wall and heard the sharp crack of a bone breaking.

When Big Sid yelped and sucked his bloody knuckles, Tennant thought, *Now we're both single-fisted!* He endeavored to slip past Stromberg, wanting room enough for the fast footwork which would neutralize Big Sid's longer reach and heavier weight; but Stromberg clubbed him back with his right fist, exclaiming, "Oh, no you don't!"

Tennant fell against the bar, used it to propel himself forward into a clinch. He tied up Stromberg's good arm with his own good arm and tried for a body blow with his right, but there was no strength in it and the punch was useless. Stromberg stomped on Tennant's instep; when the pain of that punishment failed to loosen Tennant's grip, Big Sid tried a vicious kick with his knee, aiming it at Tennant's groin, but Tennant squirmed sideways, taking the smash on his hip. Then Stromberg put all his weight on Tennant and barged ahead, carrying the tall Texan along and jamming him hard against the wall.

There was a moment then, while Tennant gasped for air and Big Sid tore loose, when the fight seemed finished. Tennant's part of it, at least. Stromberg used his left elbow to pin Tennant against the wall; he bragged, "Now you get your needings," and was pounding him unmercifully when Tennant drove a knee into Stromberg's groin.

Big Sid groaned. He bent over, grabbing himself, and he was like that when Tennant hit him hard just below the right ear.

Whereupon Stromberg tipped over with a wooshing sigh. . . .

"You whupped him, by godfreys!" Joe Barlow exclaimed in a disbelieving voice. "You whupped him cold!"

Riding easy and enjoying the sun's increasing warmth on his shoulders, Johnny Peebles reached Menafee Camp around nine o'clock. Dude Finn was in the corral doctoring a gored bronc; he called, "Howdy, kid — you come to take my place a spell?"

"No," Johnny said, not liking to be called "kid" and showing his resentment by riding on.

"What the hell's your rush?" Finn demanded. "A feller don't git to see nobody on these one-man jobs. Worse'n bein' a goddam sheep-herder."

"I got work to do," Johnny said, without looking back.

He had never cottoned to Finn anyway. Dude was always running off at the mouth about girls. According to his say, Dude had honey-fussed with every good-looking girl in Bunchgrass Basin at one time or another. "They all like their sweetnin'," Dude had told Johnny. "It's just a question of how you go about it. Some likes to be teased and some likes to be toughed. But they'll come to a man if he handles 'em right." And Dude was always bragging about the fancy women he'd stayed with; to hear him jawbone you'd think he had spent most of his life in Mayme Shay's place.

Ed wasn't like Dude at all — scarcely ever looked at a girl, unless he was drinking. And he hadn't boozed much until he took over the Roman Four job. It wasn't seemly to stick a man in a line camp by himself, but Idaho Cleek claimed Usher couldn't afford two-man camps on account of paying the same as fighting wages the year around. TU paid good wages, all right; but being by himself so much had made a lone drinker out of Ed, and that was why he'd acted so sweet on Rose Barlow. Ed didn't give a hoot for her, nor any other female.

Johnny remembered what his brother had said the night they celebrated Johnny's eighteenth birthday by calling on the girls at Mayme Shay's place. Ed had bought him a drink to warm him up and take away the shy feeling a feller gets the first time he walks into a pleasure parlor. Afterward Ed had asked him if he felt like a growed-up man, and then he'd said, "Women are just like bartenders, Johnny. They make a feller feel ten foot tall while his money lasts, but when you're broke they look down their nose as if you was a runty bum knee deep in a boghole." Then Ed had told about his swell scheme for saving up a stake and buying a ranch of their own in Texas. Just thinking about it now made Johnny feel good. . . .

"We'll have our own brand — the EJ Connected," he mused. "Which is more'n Pardee or Naviska'll ever have."

There'd be no more bunkhouse jokes about honey-fussin' females then, or being called "kid" all the time; no more lonely line-camp jobs for Ed. They'd live in their own house and brand their own cattle and maybe have the fastest damn quarter horse in seven counties.

Johnny saw half a dozen head of TU steers in the timber beyond Menafee Camp, but he didn't bother to chouse them out. Time enough for that after he'd hooked up with Ed. A galoot got lonesome for his kinfolk when he didn't see them for a longish spell. Johnny put his horse to a lope, and leaving the trail, took a short cut through the roughs southwest of the Pot Holes. This, he thought, was hellish country to work cattle in — all up and down and yonderly. Texas was the place; a man could ride all day on the Panhandle plains and never see a hill. These Arizona cow-pokes could have this Godforsaken country and welcome to it.

When he crossed the last ridge above Roman Four Johnny glimpsed the burned cabin, and smelled it. "What the hell!" he blurted.

Then, remembering what Cleek had said about Ben Petty hating Ed's guts, Johnny rushed his bronc down the ridge. If that damn home-steader had hurt Ed, or run him off. . . .

He was thinking about that, and half afraid he might find Ed wounded or something, when he galloped up to the great gray mound of ashes and saw what remained of Ed, sprawled between the charred uprights of the doorway.

"God A'mighty!" Johnny whispered.

5. Whose Boots?

Windy Biddle was gingerly shaving Tennant's tough beard and expressing his enthusiastic opinion of the fist fight so recently ended, when Sheriff Sam Lambert strode into the barbershop. The old lawman came over to the chair, peered at Tennant's lathered face and said, "So you're back."

Tennant waited until Biddle lifted the razor; then he said, "Yeah."

Lambert squirted tobacco juice into a cuspidor, and wiped his down-swirling mustache on the back of an age-mottled hand. "Word reached me at the cattle pens that a fight was goin' on," he reported.

Tennant looked up at Biddle who stood over him with razor poised. "You hear anything about a fight?" he asked.

The bald-headed barber blinked. He swallowed, and shook his head and said nothing; which was a miracle of restraint, considering his reputation for free and fancy talking.

"Must've been a false rumor," Tennant suggested soberly.

"Sid Stromberg don't look like he was hit by no false rumor," Lambert said in a mildly complaining voice. "He looks like he got tromped by a bronc."

That was enough for Windy Biddle. "What a

fight!" he exclaimed. "Blood all over the place. Sid pounding Jeff back and back, step by step, knocking him against the bar!"

Windy's eyes popped, seeing it all again. He waved his arms, narrowly missing the brim of Lambert's hat with the razor. "It seemed as if Jeff was licked — as if he didn't have a prayer. But you should of saw the way he finished him off, Sam — with one terrific blow that flattened Big Sid like a busted bag!"

Lambert, who had stepped beyond range of the waving razor, said to Tennant, "That's a poor way to make a fresh start, son. A tol'able poor way."

"Fresh start hell," Tennant scoffed. Then he said, "It might interest you to know I found Ed Peebles smothered to death in my cabin about sundown yesterday."

"Judas priest!" Windy Biddle exclaimed.

Lambert said, "Smothered?" and repeated it, as if the word were strange to him, "Smothered?"

Tennant nodded. "By all the signs Ed went to bed drunk with a lit cigarette."

Lambert shifted his tobacco cud from one jaw to the other. "You sure he smothered? You sure about that?"

"Yes," Tennant said, guessing what was in Lambert's mind. "I'm positive."

Johnny Peebles came in then. His face was pale and there was a sick look in his eyes. "Ben Petty murdered my brother," he announced.

Sheriff Lambert's glance shifted from Peebles

to Tennant and back again. "What makes you so sure Ed was murdered?" he demanded.

"I got eyes," Johnny said. "I ain't blind."

He hitched up his belt and looked at his boots and said, "There's a bullet hole in the back of Ed's head. I found horse tracks leading from Petty's corral to the burned cabin and back again."

Lambert looked at Tennant. "I thought you said —"

But Tennant asked Johnny, "How come you rode to Roman Four this morning?"

"Cleek sent me up there to help Ed," Johnny said.

Tennant thought, *The dirty dog, sending a kid to see a thing like that!* Yet even as this resentment ran through him, he felt a sense of satisfaction in the thought that Cleek and Usher had over-played their hands. Sending Johnny to Roman Four might take some explaining before it would stand as coincidence. An inquisitive jury might wonder why Cleek should have picked this par-ticular day to have Johnny help his brother; a smart lawyer might ask Johnny if he'd ever re-ceived such an assignment before, and the answer might be "no."

"Petty is hidin' out in the hills," Johnny said to Lambert. "It'll take a posse to corral him."

Lambert nodded, and Windy Biddle exclaimed, "I'll get a horse from the livery and go with you!"

"Not until you finish shaving me, you won't," Tennant told him. "This is one time you're going to take care of business before pleasure."

"Time's awastin'," Johnny complained impatiently. "We'd best be ridin', Sheriff."

Lambert went to the doorway, stopping there in the hesitant fashion of a man not sure of himself. There was a harassed expression in his eyes; indecision plainly nagged him. Here was a man, Tennant guessed, who had made many mistakes and learned little from them. Some of those mistakes had turned him timid in the face of trouble, so that now he was like an old team horse astraddle of a trace chain and not knowing which way to jump. . . .

Lambert said, "You stay in town till I git back, Tennant. I'll want some more talk from you."

"Sure," Tennant agreed. "All the talk you want." And as Lambert departed with Johnny Peebles, Tennant added, "Maybe more talk than you'll want to hear."

"What you mean by that?" Biddle asked inquisitively.

Tennant ignored the question. He glanced through a side window at the clock atop the courthouse belfry, noting the time. "I dislike to hurry a man," he said solemnly and drew his gun, "but if I'm not shut of these whiskers in ten minutes I'm going to make a target of every mirror, shaving mug and tonic bottle in this place."

"Judas priest," Windy muttered, and thereafter plied his razor with such diligence that Tennant was crossing the Senate Hotel veranda eight minutes later.

Billy Barlow, who was fourteen years old and tall for his age, greeted Tennant with a grin. "That was a dandy fight you won," he declared.

Tennant eyed him appraisingly and said, "You've sure put on some height since I saw you. Reckon you must be around sixteen or seventeen by now."

Billy blushed with pleasure, not correcting that estimate. He asked, "You going to need any help out to your place, Jeff?" And while Tennant was considering how to answer, Billy added, "I still got my saddle and rope, and I can ride better'n the last time you saw me work cattle."

"How about your job here at the hotel?" Tennant inquired.

Billy puckered his lips and spat over the veranda railing and announced disgustedly, "This piddlin' outfit ain't no fit place for a ranch-raised feller. Town life is a sorry way to live, Jeff."

"Shouldn't wonder," Tennant agreed, remembering how he had rebelled at spending his life in a law office for similar reasons. He had tried to make his father understand those reasons, telling him about the hungers no amount of food could dispel — the nostalgia that nagged a range-bred man every time he passed a saddle shop, or saw a cowboy tote his war bag into a hotel, or heard steers bawling in a stockyard pen; about the remembered feel of a good horse bracing against the rope jolt of a caught cow — all the sights and sounds and smells a man experienced working cattle, and in no other way. But his father, who'd spent forty years asaddle and envied any man that earned his living on foot, had glumly predicted, "You'll be just another fiddle-footed fool making horse tracks in the dust."

"Reckon you could use a hand?" Billy asked hopefully.

"I might later on," Tennant admitted, "when things get straightened out a trifle."

Billy smiled knowingly. "Guess I know what you got in mind," he said, eyeing Tennant's gun. "Maw spooked Dad into quittin' the cow business, but there ain't nobody going to spook you off'n your ranch, are they, Jeff?"

Tennant shook his head. He asked, "You reckon it's too late for me to get some dinner?"

"Just pick yourself a table," Billy said and started for the kitchen. "I'll send Rose right in to take your order."

Tennant went into the dining room and sat down. Doc Medwick, he guessed, should have left Roman Four by now. The old medico might meet Lambert and Johnny Peebles on his way home; but he might not, depending on the time element, for the sheriff and Johnny would cut cross country once they got into the Tailholts, and so might miss Medwick. Which would simplify things all around. . . .

Rose Barlow came into the dining room and looked at Tennant with a frank, almost brazen, interest. Her black hair, fashioned high on her head, made her look taller than she was; her red-checked gingham dress fitted snugly at the waist, accentuating well-rounded breasts. She had pouty lips; *kissing lips,* Tennant reflected, and dark flirty eyes that invited a man's attention. She said in a thoroughly pleased voice, "I'm awfully glad you're back, Jeff."

Tennant thought, *Showing me she's a town girl now,* and understood why Ed Peebles had got fresh with her. And why Ben Petty had taken up target practice. A girl like Rose would keep a man busy defending her honor.

"Three years prettier than the last time I saw you," Tennant said by way of pleasing her.

He had remained seated; but now, as Mrs. Barlow came in wiping flour-dusted hands on her apron, Tennant stood up and bowed in gallant fashion and asked, "Do you still bake the best corn bread in Arizona, ma'am?"

"I see you haven't lost your glib tongue for the girls, young or old," Effie Barlow said disdainfully. But she couldn't quite hide her appreciation, revealing it in the way she compressed her lips against smiling. She glanced critically at Rose and asked, "Why, in heaven's name, don't you bring the man some food instead of standing there gawking at him? He looks like he'd been drug through a knothole."

The thought came to Tennant that there was scarcely any resemblance between this faded, flat-bosomed woman and her sultry-eyed daughter. It seemed downright odd that such a careworn woman should have mothered a girl like Rose, or that so wilted a man as Joe Barlow should have sired her. . . .

Rose said sullenly, "I'm no mind reader, Mother. Jeff hasn't ordered yet."

"Good gracious, girl, bring the man what we've got — beef and potatoes and a cup of coffee."

Rose took time to primp a black curl into place behind an ear. Then she asked, "Is that what you'd like, Jeff?"

"Suits me fine," Tennant said and sat down expecting that Mrs. Barlow would follow Rose to the kitchen. But instead she took a chair at the table, and when young Billy came into the room, she said sharply, "You go on about your business, son."

"But I got some things to talk over with Jeff," Billy protested.

"So have I," Effie announced. "Now go along with you."

What, Tennant wondered, could she want to talk to him about? He watched Billy sulk like a balky horse, and as the boy departed with deliberate slowness, Tennant thought, *That kid will run off one of these days to see what's over the hill.*

"My Joe is talking big about helping you drive TU out of the Tailholt Hills," Effie Barlow said.

Tennant showed his surprise by demanding, "What would give Joe an idea like that?"

Effie Barlow shrugged, and sighed, and said nervously, "I don't know what your plans are, and I don't care, just so Joe don't get mixed up in them. He's too old a man to sashay around with a — well, with a hot-blooded young hellion like you."

Tennant showed her a self-mocking smile. "An ex-convict to boot," he suggested.

"I don't care about that, one way or the other," Effie Barlow said. "Some folks say you was guilty, and some say you was framed. I don't know. And I guess the jury wouldn't of been so sure if it hadn't been TU brands that was altered. But I know that Joe has a wild streak in him. He killed a man in Texas once, before we was married. It might of meant jail for him, except that my old pappy was sheriff."

Then, as Rose came in carrying a tray, she asked softly, urgently, "Would you do me a favor, Jeff — a big favor?"

"Sure," Tennant agreed.

"Promise you won't let Joe side you, no matter what happens."

Tennant smiled, amused at the thought of her booze-fogged husband helping anyone in a fight. "It's a promise," he said.

"Thank you," Effie Barlow exclaimed, and when she reached the kitchen door she called back, "There'll be hot apple pie by the time you're ready for it."

6. A Blue Chip Bargain

Doctor Medwick drove up in front of the Senate Hotel and motioned to Billy Barlow who sat on the veranda steps. When the boy came over to Doc's buggy, Medwick asked, "Want to earn two bits, son?"

Billy considered this for a moment, not wanting to appear eager. Tay McGonigle, he had observed, never accepted an offer in a hurry when he was making a horse trade, no matter how good the bargain was. . . .

"Well," Doc asked impatiently, "do you, or don't you?"

"Sure," Billy said.

Medwick got down and handed Billy a quarter and said, "Tay McGonigle is on his way to the Tailholts with a wagon, and I haven't got time to stable Prince. Give him a fork of hay, but don't let him have any water. He's a trifle hot." Then he asked, "Is Jeff Tennant inside?"

"Eatin'," Billy reported. He had a boy's profound faith in Doc's opinions and so he asked, "You reckon Jeff could outshoot Idaho Cleek?"

Medwick took off his glasses and blew dust from their lenses. Ben Petty had asked the same question at Bar Bell this morning. Ben had seemed sure Tennant would try to kill Tate Usher, and that he'd have to fight Cleek first. It was, Doc thought now, a reasonable supposition shared by everyone who knew Jeff Tennant.

"They say no one can beat Cleek," Doc said, and went up the veranda steps.

"I bet Jeff can," Billy declared. "I bet he can do anything he puts his mind to."

Which was also a reasonable supposition, Doc reflected, considering Jeff Tennant's past performance in a variety of endeavors. The tall Texan had a habit of getting things done. Recalling how easily and quickly Tennant had displaced Clark Morgan as Jane's suitor when he first came to Quadrille, Doc felt an urgent regret. Clark had a dependable, steady-going way with him; he would have made Jane a good husband. . . .

The old medico sighed, went to the dining-room doorway and stood there for a moment, watching Rose Barlow serve Tennant his dessert. There was a coquettish smile on the girl's flushed face, and Doc noticed that she leaned close to Tennant when she placed his pie before him. Jeff, he reflected, seemed to attract women — all kinds of women.

Presently, as Doc shook hands with Tennant, he understood what Jane had told him when he'd stopped by the house on his way into town. "Jeff looks just the same, except for his eyes," Jane had said. "They're hard as rock, even when he smiles." And so they were.

Rose went back to the kitchen and Doc asked quietly, "What do you know about those bullet holes in Ed Peebles' corpse?"

"I know Peebles smothered to death long before the shots were fired," Tennant said, and told Medwick the whole story. Then he asked, "Did you get the measurements of those two boot prints near the watering trough?"

Medwick nodded. "But they don't match, Jeff. What good are they?"

"That's what I thought, three years ago," Tennant muttered. "I saw the same off-sized prints at the stockyard gate where a brand-blotting deal was framed on me. And they were fresh made. But I thought they were the tracks of different men. Now I know they belong to one man."

"Who?" Doc asked.

Tennant shrugged. "They might belong to most anybody," he said. "But you can damn soon find out."

"How?" Medwick demanded, entirely puzzled.

Tennant finished off the generous wedge of apple pie, and Doc asked, "You aren't planning to kill Tate Usher, are you?"

"Yes," Tennant said in the most matter-of-fact voice a man could use. "I intended to do it the first time he came to town, but now I'll have to wait until we clear Ben Petty. There's a certain question Usher should be asked at Ben's trial, and he couldn't answer it if he was dead."

Doc said, "Killing Usher wouldn't give you back those three years at Yuma, Jeff. It would just mean more trouble, all round."

A cynical smile slanted Tennant's lean face.

"The world," he mused, "is full of trouble. Especially Bunchgrass Basin."

"How about identifying the boot prints?" Medwick asked.

"Dutch Vedder makes boots for most of the men in this country," Tennant explained. "He keeps a foot book with the exact outlines of his customers' feet, right and left. As coroner you've got a legal right to examine that book, and compare the measurements."

Medwick peered thoughtfully at Tennant. He said, "Usher and Cleek passed me on the road at dusk yesterday. They might've taken the side trail to Roman Four afterward. If either one of them made those prints you'd have something definite to offer as evidence that your story is true."

"Yeah," Tennant agreed, "something a thick-headed jury might understand, in case Ben Petty is arrested for murder. But keep it quiet, Doc. Don't let Lambert know about it, or anyone else."

"All right," Doc said. "I'll go take a look at Vedder's book."

Then a new thought struck him and he exclaimed, "Say — if we prove Usher framed Petty we'd know he also framed you!"

"And how surprised we'd all be," Tennant said mockingly.

When Medwick went into the lobby, Tennant heard Big Sid Stromberg say, "I been looking for you, Doc. My hand is all swelled up and feels like there's a broken bone. My nose feels the same way."

They went on outside then, and Tennant wondered how long Big Sid had been in the lobby, and how much he had heard of the conversation. Tennant went quickly to the lobby and asked Joe Barlow who was lounging there, "How long was Stromberg here before Doc came out?"

"Not more'n a minute or two," Joe said. "He'd just got back from a trip to Doc's house."

Tennant loosed a sigh of relief. The mismatched boot angle wouldn't be worth much if Usher heard about it before the trial. It was the only shred of evidence that could be offered to show that TU's boss had stopped at Roman Four last night, and it would be effective only if Usher denied stopping there. . . .

"I'm staying in town for a few days," Tennant said. "How about fixing me up with a front room?"

"Sure, sure — anything you want," Joe declared, and when he handed Tennant the key, he asked softly, "When you goin' to start puttin' the run on that TU bunch, Jeff?"

"What gave you that idea?" Tennant inquired.

Barlow winked grinningly. "Just puttin' two and two together and makin' 'em equal Roman Four. I heard Leona Bell is going to drive TU off Tonto Flats, and that Ben Petty is goin' to help her. That means fightin' in the Tailholts, which means you'll be in on it."

Then he lowered his voice again, and said,

"That's my country, too, Jeff. I shouldn't of ever left it. I'm throwin' in with you and Ben and Leona Bell when the shootin' starts."

So that's why Ellie wanted me to make her a promise, Tennant reflected. He chuckled, thinking how ridiculous a setup Joe was suggesting: a girl-bossed crew, a fugitive homesteader and a booze-befuddled old cowman, stacked up against TU's tough gun-hawk bunch.

"I guess you got your reports mixed up," Tennant told him. "I don't think Ben Petty will be helping Bar Bell, and neither will I. We'll be too busy helping ourselves."

Then, because the bruised knuckles of his hands were sore and beginning to swell, he went out to the kitchen and announced, "I could use a pitcher of real hot water."

Ten minutes later, as he stood at the washstand soaking his hands in steaming water, Leona Bell came to the doorway of his room and said in friendly fashion, "Without your whiskers you look exactly like Jeff Tennant."

Her smile was good to see, and when he said, "Without your scowl you look exactly like Leona Bell," her tinkling laughter was good to hear. It was a surprising thing. She was wearing the same riding clothes she'd worn yesterday, but she seemed to be a different person — a cheerful, gracious sister of the haughty girl he had met at Commissary Creek.

Leona came into the room and glanced at his hands and said, "They say you gave Big Sid a proper licking. I hope you didn't cripple yourself doing it."

Tennant shook his head. "Just a trifle sore is all." He was reaching for a towel when she asked, "How would you like to own one hundred head of Bar Bell cows and five blooded bulls?"

Tennant's hand didn't reach the towel. He turned slowly and stared at her and said, "Say that again."

"How would you like to own one hundred head of young heifers and your pick of five Bar Bell bulls?"

Tennant wiped his wet hands on his pants. He took out his Durham sack and shaped up a cigarette and thought, *She means it. She means it sure as hell!*

"That," Leona said quietly, "is the price I'm willing to pay if you'll ramrod my fight against TU."

When Tennant lit his cigarette and took a long drag without speaking, she added, "Not only willing, but *glad* to pay." And she was smiling when she said it. . . .

For a moment then, as all his discarded dreams came trooping back, Jeff Tennant was tempted to say yes — to accept the offer without telling her he had already decided to kill Tate Usher. One hundred cows would give him a calf crop of around seventy-five calves the first year. That much breeder stock would put him ahead of where he would've been if he hadn't gone to Yuma; it would help pay off for Claude Bell's part in sending him to prison. But finally Tennant said, "I guess you haven't heard that I intend to kill Tate Usher."

"I've heard you intend to try it. But I'm offering you a much better proposition. Unless you plan to dry-gulch Usher you wouldn't have a chance. You'd be up against Idaho Cleek, and he's too fast for you. Even if by some miracle you managed to kill Usher and live, you'd still have nothing to show for it except some satisfaction. And you can't get far on that. Satisfaction is all right for a trail tramp whose highest ambition is to own a silver-mounted saddle. But you're no trail tramp."

Tennant grinned. "How would you know that?" he inquired.

"Ben Petty told me all about your plans to buy blooded bulls. According to him you used to have more fancy plans for the future than any ten men in the Tailholt Hills."

"So," Tennant mused, admiring her frankness, and her bargaining ability. She had picked the one inducement that would surely tempt him to change his plans; she was like a high-stake gambler pushing in a stack of blue chips.

"I have an ambition also," Leona said.

She wasn't smiling now. Yet — and Tennant couldn't understand why this was so — she was close to being beautiful when she said angrily, "I want to see TU shrunk back to its original size — to the sorry, shirttail outfit it was fifteen years ago!"

It occurred to Tennant now that he'd never considered anger in women an aid to beauty. It usually worked the other way. But this girl's anger was like a flame of pure passion, so elemental that it warmed her thoroughly, as a woman in love might be warmed. Color came swiftly into her face, her eyes took on a tawny, gold-flecked glow; even her lips seemed redder and fuller. Remembering how consistently peaceable a man her father had been, Tennant marveled that Claude Bell's daughter should be so different.

"What," he asked, "makes you think that I could accomplish the chore?"

"Because you're tough," Leona told him. "I saw it in your eyes yesterday. You've shaved off your whiskers since then, and put on a clean shirt. But you haven't changed your eyes."

Then she said, "There's another reason why I want you to ramrod the fight. It's because you despise Tate Usher almost as much as I do."

"Almost as much?" Tennant asked.

She nodded. "No one else has so much reason to despise him. You and I have kindred ambitions, Jeff, and we may both realize them — if you'll take the job."

"I still don't see why you're so sure," Tennant countered. "Even if I was an expert slug-slammer, I'd be just one more gun on your side."

"But that one gun would be to my crew what Idaho Cleek's gun is to Usher's crew. A fight like this calls for more than courage. It isn't just a case of being ready and willing to defend a ranch. That's been the trouble with Jules Huffmeyer all along; he insisted on playing the game according to the rules. But Usher doesn't play like that. He uses every trick he can think of — dirty, underhanded tricks that scare folks into letting TU hog the grass. We've got to fight him the same way, and you're the man to do it. You may not be able to match Cleek's fast draw, but your year at law school should make it easy for you to outsmart him."

She watched Tennant's slow, self-mocking smile, and liked it. "You see," she explained, "I know much more about you than I did yesterday."

"Maybe more than I knew myself, yesterday," Tennant reflected. "I didn't know I was still ambitious."

"Then you'll take the job?" Leona asked eagerly.

Tennant walked over to the window, tossed his dead cigarette into the street and began fashioning a fresh one. "Seems like you're offering a high price," he muttered, "especially when you know I planned to go gunning for Usher on my own."

Leona shook her head. "The price isn't high considering that Bar Bell will be crowded out of business unless I stop TU. In fact I stand to lose a lot of cattle this winter unless I save the graze on Tonto Flats. And as for your personal fight with Usher, well, you'd have to catch him away from Cleek, which is next to impossible. Even if you should, I doubt if Usher would fight you, man to man. Did you ever hear of him doing his own gun work?"

"No," Tennant admitted.

"Then it adds up to this," Leona went on, in the matter-of-fact tone of a merchant itemizing a bill of goods. "If you go after Usher your way you risk being killed by Cleek, without a chance of winning a thing. If you do it my way you'll be helping me save Bar Bell from sure ruin, and you'll have a chance to turn Roman Four into a well-stocked ranch. Either way you risk your hide, I'll admit — but as my ramrod you'd get paid for taking the risk."

"If Bar Bell won," Tennant pointed out. "Otherwise, no."

Leona nodded. She studied him for a long moment, as if attempting to tally the results of her argument. Then she said, "If you ask my crew what our chances are they'll ask you who Usher's bunch ever beat. Even Ben Petty thinks we've got a chance to win."

Tennant smiled. "So does Joe Barlow," he said. And afterward, as if thinking aloud, he muttered, "They might be right, at that. They just barely might be."

"There's a way you can find out for sure," Leona suggested.

"Yeah."

Leona waited out an interval of silence. Then she asked, very softly, "Will you take the job?"

"Yes," Tennant said.

It was then that Doc Medwick came to the doorway and announced, "You certainly did a job on Big Sid. He'll be tending bar one-handed a month or more."

"Too bad for the Saturday night trade," Tennant said. "Service will be slow." Then he asked, "What's the verdict, Doc?" and when Medwick glanced questioningly at Leona, Tennant said, "It's all right for her to hear. She's just hired me to ramrod Bar Bell's fight against TU."

Medwick stared at them in frank astonishment. "She has?" he demanded. Then he said wearily, "God help us all."

"Doc, you sound awfully pessimistic," Leona protested.

"What can you expect from a man who has to clean up the messes other men make?" Tennant asked. He watched Medwick take off his glasses and clean them. Doc, he reflected, had never been happy about having him court Jane; now the old medico would be even less enthusiastic. Finally Tennant asked, "Well, what did you find out?"

"The prints were made by Usher," Medwick said. "He's got mismatched feet."

7. A Man Must Eat

Fall haze lay powder blue all across the Tailholt Hills. At sundown a chill breeze came off Dragoon Divide, bringing its hint of winter to Ben Petty who was scouting the timber above his homestead. He hadn't eaten since breakfast and was hungry, but because he'd seen two riders near here an hour ago, Petty disliked the risk of obtaining food at his shack. The whole TU crew would be cruising these hills by now. . . .

Dusk came and a stronger breeze stirred the pines to restless sighing. The day's worry and waiting had rubbed Petty's nerves raw; he glanced frequently over his shoulder, and when he began a cautious circle of the clearing he drew his gun, holding it ready for the rush of riders he half expected. He made a complete turn of the clearing and halted again, not quite satisfied. Those two riders he'd glimpsed from a distance had headed toward Bar Bell; but they might have doubled back — they might be in the shack now, waiting for him to show himself. The gun's hickory handle felt slippery in his fingers; he sheathed the gun and wiped his perspiring palm against his pants and peered across the clearing. The thought came to him that he had lived alone in that cheerless shack for a long time and never known real loneliness. But he knew it now; the loneliest feeling a man could have: the feeling of being hunted.

For a time then, as Ben Petty waited for his courage to equal his hunger, fragmentary impressions of the day's occurrences came back to him: Jeff Tennant's scoffing declaration that the truth was too simple; Leona Bell's surprise at learning of Tennant's return, and the pleased way she'd said, "So that's who I met yesterday!" And Doc Medwick's worried voice as he drove off toward Roman Four saying, "There'll be hell to pay."

Recalling how he'd been tempted to tell the old medico about the bullet holes, Petty wondered if he'd done right by following Jeff Tennant's peculiar instructions. Jeff had a tough and cocksure way with him; he'd always been a high-riding galoot. Going to jail, Ben guessed, hadn't changed him much, except to make him tougher. Perhaps it would've been better to tell Doc Medwick the whole story, straight out.

Petty was worrying about that when he heard horses come down the slope north of his shack. A breeze was blowing directly toward him and so the sound of travel was plain even though the horses were some distance away. His first impulse was to ride in swift retreat; he was whirling his bronc when he heard another rider off to the west. That halted him at once. It meant they were spread out; it meant he might run into more riders coming from the east and south. Petty shivered, drew his gun, and heard Tate Usher call, "That you, Idaho?"

75

Cleek's muttered reply came from a point close to the shack, and another man — Petty thought it sounded like Red Naviska — declared, "He wouldn't dillydally around here. Bar Bell is the place to watch, and them homesteads in the Bandoleers."

"We split up and watch 'em all," Idaho Cleek announced, "after we have us a bait of food."

Ben Petty listened for sound of travel behind him. Presently he heard Dude Finn inquire, "You plannin' to catch Petty — or kill him?"

Ben waited, wanting to hear the answer, and shivered a little when Tate Usher proclaimed, "Shoot him down on sight, just like he shot poor Ed!"

"That's all I need to know," Finn said happily. "I never liked that jigger, no how."

Ben cursed softly. Dude was another one who'd acted fresh with Rose; another smart-alecky son too big for his britches. There was more talk, but Ben didn't wait to hear it. He eased his horse deeper into the pines; when he looked back there was lamplight at the shack, and later, as he rimmed the ridge, the light still showed. Those men would soon be eating supper, filling their bellies at his table and with his food. The hunger grind in Petty's stomach got worse; he wondered where Sheriff Lambert and the other TU riders were. They might be anywhere, watching any trail, waiting for him to make a move. He held his gun ready, and rode toward Quadrille. A man had to eat. . . .

8. "Ride Off, Ben — Ride Off!"

Supper was over, the dishes washed and put away; and Doc Medwick had departed, saying something about a friendly poker game. Tennant sat with Jane on the front porch, watching the way window lamplight revealed the contours of her face each time she turned her head to look directly at him. She was, he decided, more lovely than she'd been three years ago; more womanly, and therefore more desirable. He felt for her hand and found it, and said, "It's good to be back."

"Good to have you back," Jane murmured. During supper she had listened without comment to her father's pessimistic predictions regarding Bar Bell's chances against TU. Now she said, "So you're to be Leona's fighting foreman."

There was no censure in her voice. But there was no pleasure in it either, and Tennant asked, "Any objections, ma'am?"

Jane shook her head. "I've no right to object."

It was, he knew, her way of reminding him that there'd been no definite understanding between them. He said, "It's a chance to settle my score with Usher. I'd planned to do it in a more direct and quicker way, but Ben Petty's mix-up changed that. Ben branded calves for me, and so I'm trying to return his favor. There's only one way to clear him of Peebles' murder — by having

Tate Usher testify that he wasn't at Roman Four last night, and then proving he was."

"I can understand all that," Jane said. "But I can't understand how Leona Bell could talk you into becoming a hired gun-slinger — even for one hundred head of cattle."

Tennant shrugged. He didn't entirely understand it himself. It was, he guessed, a combination of things: the fact that he'd had to alter his original plans because of Ben Petty, and the realization that Usher probably couldn't be goaded into a gun duel. But the real reason was the bait Leona Bell had used, the bargain that had renewed his discarded dreams. . . .

"I'm gambling my time for a big bunch of cattle," he said, knowing how flimsy an explanation this must sound to Jane.

"You're gambling your reputation," she reminded him, "and perhaps your life."

Tennant chuckled. "Do you think being Bar Bell's ramrod would hurt a brand-blotter's reputation? Don't forget that I'm an ex-convict, Jane — a culprit who's paid his debt to society. Nine hundred and sixty-five days of debt, with four months off for good behavior."

"I know, Jeff, and I don't blame you for being bitter. It's — well, it doesn't seem like you to fight for pay."

"According to Doc's predictions, I'm not," Tennant said. "If Bar Bell loses there won't be any pay."

For a time then, while Jane sat with her face

78

half shadowed and half lighted, Tennant studied the profile of her lips, deliberately tantalizing himself with their remembered sweetness and what they could do to him. They weren't shaped in a cupid's bow like Rose Barlow's lips; they had a longer, softer curve that was more pleasantly expressive. Idly comparing her with Rose, Tennant understood another thing about this oval-faced girl who sat so quietly beside him. There was a quality in Jane that made a man remember his manners, a sort of obscure dignity, so that she could look a man in the eye and understand what he was thinking, and not blush. And not seem brazen, either.

Jane turned her head and said, "A penny for your thoughts."

"I was thinking," Tennant told her, "how nice it would be to kiss you?"

"So?"

Afterward, while he held her in his arms and felt the lessening pressure her breathing made against his chest, Tennant knew again what he'd known the first time he kissed her: Jane had an outward calm that was like the smooth flow of deep-running water unruffled by all the turbulence below its surface. There were strong currents of emotion in her — a flood tide of affection waiting for the man she married.

"Another penny for your thoughts," Jane offered.

"The man was thinking how much he'd like to ask the girl to marry him," Tennant said. "The man was telling himself it would be the first thing he'd do when he owns a fitting home for so beautiful a bride."

He watched the way her slow smile gently curved her lips. He heard the remote rumor of a horse somewhere west of the Big Arroyo bridge, and was wondering about its rider when Jane said softly, "The girl isn't particular about the house. It's the man she'd be marrying and there's no reason for him to be overly proud about worldly goods, one way or the other."

Tennant kissed her again, long and hard. He breathed in the feminine scent of her hair, knowing it was the most delicious perfume he'd ever smelled — the most intimate. He kissed the tip of her nose, and her right ear, and the soft hollow below it. . . .

Afterward, as horse tromp bonged on the bridge planks, he said, "I'm going to have a real ranch when I ask a girl to marry me — or I'll not be asking."

Then Ben Petty halted his horse in the long shaft of lamplight and called nervously, "Is Jeff Tennant there?"

Tennant went out to the gate and demanded, "What you doing here, Ben?"

"They got me shut off from my shack and from Bar Bell," Petty reported. "I'm going to get some grub at the Senate. Sheriff Sam ain't come back, has he?"

"Haven't seen him," Tennant said.

"I passed Tay McGonigle up the road a piece.

He says Kid Peebles swore out a warrant for me, and Sam seems to think I killed Ed. Would your story clear me, Jeff, when you tell all of it?"

Tennant nodded.

Whereupon Petty smiled and said, "Then mebbe I'd best give myself up, if you're sure."

"I'm not sure at all," Tennant said quickly, wanting to emphasize this. "Usher might be smart enough to spoil our ace in the hole, and there's no telling what a jury will do. Look what they did to me. No, Ben, I'm not sure at all."

Petty thought about this, looking worried, and rubbed a thumb up and down his bristled chin. "Damn if I know what to do," he mumbled. "If I give myself up they might convict me of murder. If I don't, one of them TU slugslammers is liable to shoot me down like a dog."

The sound of a wagon came from the quilted darkness west of Big Arroyo then, and Petty said, "That's McGonigle, bringin' in Peebles' remains." He buttoned his denim jacket and said, "Nights are gittin' cold." He listened to the wagon as it rumbled across the bridge; then he asked, "Whet would you do, Jeff?"

Tennant frowned, not liking this. He thought, *I'd make them hunt me down, and maybe I'd do some hunting myself. It'd be fight and run and fight some more.* But Ben Petty wasn't much of a fighter. The lanky, loose-jointed homesteader had lost his urge for conflict the moment he learned of Ed Peebles' death. Lacking a motive for revenge, or for protecting Rose Barlow's honor, he had no strong prop against the increasing pressure of apprehension and discomfort. . . .

"I'd probably make 'em catch me," Tennant said.

The wagon came closer, its wheels rolling quietly through the road's deep dust. Petty said, "If I could make it to Hobo Bill's place up under the Rim they'd never get me. Guess that's where I'll head for first thing tomorrow morning. I'm tireder'n six Sonora steers and twice as hungry."

"I'll fix you some supper in a jiffy," Jane called from the veranda.

Petty shook his head. "Thanks just the same, ma'am, but — well, I sort of wanted to see Rose."

Tennant grinned. Ben, he guessed, would never be too tired or hungry or worried to visit Rose Barlow. "You'd better ride down Sashay Alley," he suggested, "and go into the hotel by the kitchen door."

"Sure," Ben agreed, and was climbing to saddle when McGonigle's team came into the shaft of lamplight.

Tennant called, "Howdy, Tay," and at this same instant Sheriff Lambert jumped from the wagon, spooking Ben's bronc against the fence.

Tennant said, "Ride off, Ben — ride off!"

But Petty took a moment to think about this, and then Lambert rushed up and announced, "You're under arrest!"

Petty went altogether slack in saddle. He said, "I didn't have a thing to do with Peebles' death. Honest I didn't."

"That's the jury's chore," Lambert muttered. "Climb down, Ben. I'm taking you to jail."

Tennant had stepped back along the fence so that he was out of the lamplight. Now he said, "You might be wrong about that, Sam."

"Wrong how?" Lambert demanded, peering into the darkness where Tennant stood.

"All wrong," Tennant said. He glanced at Petty; seeing how dejectedly Ben slumped, and said, "You don't have to go with him."

There was a moment when the breathing of McGonigle's road-weary team was a plain sound; when Jane, standing on the veranda steps, heard the slight creak of leather as Ben Petty straightened in his saddle. Then Sheriff Lambert shouted, "Oh, yes he does!"

And the loudness of the lawman's voice told Jane that Lambert was afraid. . . .

She looked at Jeff, seeing his high, indistinct shape in the shadows, by the fence. She thought, *He has no right to interfere,* and heard Jeff say, "Not unless you want to, Ben. Not unless you want to."

It was a strange thing. Lambert ignored Ben completely. He kept peering at Jeff, his head canted to one side and his right hand close to holster. "You try interferin' and I'll take you to jail with him," Lambert warned.

"I guess not," Tennant said in a quiet, almost casual tone. "I guess you'll never take me in for anything."

Jane held her breath, expecting Lambert to

83

draw his gun, and fearing that Jeff would shoot him if he did. It didn't occur to her that Jeff might be hurt if this came to a showdown. There was just one thought in her mind now, and one fear — the awful fear of seeing Jeff shoot Sheriff Lambert. She tried to tell herself that Jeff was bluffing, that he wouldn't kill a blundering old man who was merely doing his duty. But she kept remembering how the hardness stayed in Jeff's eyes, even when he smiled. . . .

She called urgently, "Ben, why don't you go along with him!"

And she loosed a gusty sigh as Ben dismounted, saying meekly, "I'll go, Sam — but I'd like to stop by the hotel for supper."

"Sure, sure," Lambert agreed, plainly pleased to turn away from Tennant. "Just tie your bronc behind Tay's wagon with mine, and we'll go eat."

Presently, when Lambert and Petty walked down Main Street and McGonigle's wagon followed them, Tennant came back to the veranda. "Ben," he muttered, "is probably better off in jail. He won't have to decide anything there. They'll do it for him."

Then he added, "Damn a man who won't grab a good chance when he gets it."

Jane watched him shape up a cigarette and light it, his face showing a deep frown in the match flare. She asked, "But why should Ben run if he's innocent? Why should he live like a hunted thing and risk being shot?"

"Because that's better than being in prison, or tromping thin air with a rope around your neck," Tennant said.

Jane thought about that, wanting to see his side of it; wanting to believe he was right. But she recalled how Sheriff Lambert had looked, standing there with his splayed fingers close to holster. The old lawman had been trapped between fear and pride, and there'd been no doubt in his mind about Jeff bluffing. Lambert had been afraid. Afraid of dying. . . .

Tennant asked, "Did Judge Maffitt beat Luke Randall again in the last election?"

Jane nodded, watching his lamplit face ease into a smile. "Why does that please you, Jeff?"

"Because Ben needs a lawyer who has reason to dislike Tate Usher," Tennant said cheerfully. He took her arm and escorted her toward the gate. "I'd better line up Randall right now," he said. "Be leaving town early in the morning."

"Going to your new job so soon?" Jane asked, showing her disappointment in the way her fingers tightened on his arm.

Tennant nodded.

They were at the gate now, and Jane said, "You really think there's a chance for you to win those cattle, don't you, Jeff?"

"Sure," Tennant agreed, and because he didn't want her to worry about him, he used Leona's argument to prove his point. "Usher's gun-toting toughs have never licked anyone. They've bluffed their way through every deal, without a fight. We're going to ram the bluff right down their throats and make 'em eat it."

A wistful smile dimpled Jane's lamplit cheeks. "You remind me of a poem I once read, Jeff. It goes something like this: Rebels ride proudly in the sun, counting the battle already won."

"Nice," Tennant praised. He traced the sweet, full curve of her lips with a forefinger and said, "Nice enough to kiss."

Doc Medwick came home shortly after ten o'clock and found Jane alone on the veranda. "I thought Jeff would be here," Doc said, plainly disappointed.

"He went to see Lawyer Randall about defending Ben Petty," Jane reported. "Jeff is leaving for Bar Bell first thing in the morning." Then she asked, "Something special you wanted to tell him, Dad?"

"Yes, dammit. I want to warn him he's got off on the wrong foot around here. Lambert is all spooked up; he's saying Jeff threatened to draw a gun on him. Did Jeff do that?"

"Well, I suppose it amounted to a threat," Jane admitted reluctantly, and told what had transpired out there by the fence. Then she asked in a thoroughly subdued voice, "Do you think Jeff was bluffing?"

Instead of answering, Doc asked, "Do you?"

Jane was silent for a long moment. Then she said slowly, "I don't know, Dad. I just don't know," and something in her voice prompted

Doc Medwick to place an arm around her.

"I guess there always was a wild streak in Jeff," he muttered. "Three years in prison brought it to the surface, and God only knows what will cure it."

They went into the lamplit parlor and when Doc saw his daughter's eyes he said, "No man is worth the salt in one of your tears, baby. Not one."

Jeff Tennant was also the topic of conversation at Bar Bell, where Jules Huffmeyer and his five-man crew listened to Leona's announcement of Tennant's hiring. "He'll be here tomorrow," she said, "to take complete charge of things until TU is pushed back where it belongs."

Huffmeyer, who sat rigidly straight because of his tight-bound ribs, said sourly, "Tennant never struck me as bein' overly tough. It'll take more'n a smart-alecky galoot with a gun to run this ruckus, once it starts."

And Bravo Shafter, who'd been acting as straw boss since Jule's accident, muttered, "Seems odd for us to be takin' orders from a Tailholt Hills homesteader, ma'am. Tol'able odd."

"But you'll take them, regardless," Leona said confidently. "And you'll find out soon enough that he's the man to give them."

A reflective smile brought its brief change to her face and she added, "Jeff Tennant is tough, through and through."

9. Trouble Aplenty

Well fortified with one of Effie Barlow's bounteous breakfasts and by Tay McGonigle's generous application of horse liniment to his bruised
shoulder, Jeff Tennant saddled his sorrel gelding
before sunup.

" 'Tis the one regret of me life that I missed
seein' ye rock Big Sid to sleep yesterday,"
McGonigle complained. And presently, as Tennant led his horse out to the street, the liveryman
warned, "Keep an eye peeled for them TU
toughs, Jeff. They'll gang up on ye, first chance
they git."

Tennant grinned. "I could whip Usher's
bunch with a broom handle this morning," he
declared. Then he asked, "Will you do me a little
favor, Tay?"

"And why the divil wouldn't I?"

"Then stop by the jail soon as they open the
front door, and tell Ben to keep his lip buttoned
tight until Lawyer Randall comes in to see him."

"Consider it done," Tay said.

Whereupon Tennant rode west on Main
Street, sitting tall in the saddle and feeling better
than he'd felt for many a day. Part of this exuber-
ance, he knew, was the result of his talk with
Luke Randall last night. The lawyer, who'd been
defeated in three successive elections by the
narrow margin of TU's votes going to Judge

88

Maffitt, had displayed a frank eagerness to take Ben's case. And he had seemed highly optimistic about the evidence. . . .

When he passed Doc Medwick's white house, Tennant gave it a lingering regard, savoring the pleasant memories this place held for him. Jane, he guessed, wouldn't be greatly influenced by her father's pessimistic predictions. She had a mind of her own. She'd showed that four years ago when she went against her father's choice of Clark Morgan as a prospective son-in-law. Tennant grinned, recalling how meekly the mercantile proprietor had stepped aside. Morgan might know all there was to know about making money on foot, and saying no at the right time, but he sure had a lot to learn when it came to winning a wife.

The sorrel bronc settled down to the leisurely, established pace of a long-trail traveler. First sunlight spilled over the eastern rim of the basin; dew made a tinseled sparkle on the grass and a gentle breeze brought the thin-spiced scent of pine from timbered hills. For the first time in three years, Tennant whistled a cheery tune. This, he reflected, was the way it used to be. He'd always felt high as a windmill when he rode out in the morning. If it were chilly and a bronc pitched with him he'd whoop and holler for the sheer joy of being where he wanted to be and doing what he wanted to do. No ride had been too long, no work too hard in those days. He had dreamed big dreams and worked like hell to make them materialize — until a range hog's scheme stopped him.

Tennant ceased his whistling. He said, "Tate Usher," in the whispering way of a man uttering a curse. The mere mention of Usher's name curdled his thoughts; it dimmed the morning sunlight and spoiled the air he breathed. Recalling Leona Bell's assertion that he despised Usher almost as much as she did, Tennant thought, *She couldn't hate him any more than I do, and she could have no more reason for hating him.* Seeing Usher's ill-gotten spread shrunk back to shirttail size might be enough for her, but it wouldn't satisfy him. It wouldn't erase the memory of those nine hundred and sixty-five days in Yuma Prison, nor cancel out Mac Menafee's death, nor Joe Barlow's shame.

The sorrel held steadily to his running walk, hoofs scuffing the road's powdery dust. He had a habit of traveling with his ears back, as if perpetually resenting the burden he carried, and because of this characteristic, Tennant had named him "Sulky." Now Tennant noticed that Sulky's ears were tipped forward. Halting at once, Tennant listened, and heard nothing. But the sorrel kept its ears pricked and so Tennant waited, keening the crisp morning air. The thought came to him that Usher's riders wouldn't know that Ben was in jail and so they'd continue to search for him.

Tennant scanned the country ahead without finding any sign of riders, but he waited, relying entirely on the sorrel's continuing alertness. This was some six miles west of town, in a rock-jumbled stretch of desert where saguaro cactus grew tall above patches of prickly pear and greasewood. He shaped up a cigarette and had it half smoked when he caught the sharp flash of sunlight slanting off metal. Presently he glimpsed three hats above the brush; watching them come toward him he saw that one hat band was decorated with silver conchas, and recalled that Tate Usher invariably wore such an ornamented band. . . .

Tennant backed his horse against a rock outcrop at the roadside. He watched the three riders come into full view, identifying Tate Usher, Idaho Cleek and Red Naviska. It occurred to him that this wasn't the way he'd hoped to meet Usher. And in the brief interval between the time they saw him and then recognized him Tennant realized how correct Leona Bell's prediction had been. A man-to-man meeting with Usher would be little less than miraculous. There'd probably never be a time when that fat and flabby and hog-jowled man would ride alone, or walk alone, or fight alone.

"So you're back!" Usher exclaimed.

His eyes, deeply recessed in pouchy folds of flesh, were like bright blue marbles in a slot. There was no sign of embarrassment at this meeting with the man he had tricked into prison, nor any regret. Anger poured its scalding heat into Tennant's veins while he considered this, and for a moment he just sat there, peering at the living image of his long-nourished hatred. Then he said, "I came back to kill a hog, Usher — a hog just about your size and shape."

The TU boss put up a thick-palmed hand in a defensive gesture that was pure mockery. He leaned half out of saddle in a clownish portrayal of cringing fear and cried in a quavering, high-pitched voice, "Mercy me, whatever shall I do!"

Then a derisive smile rutted his heavy cheeks and he asked blandly, "Was that a threat, or just an insult?"

And then he laughed.

Tennant's hatred now was a physical thing. It was like a hunger grind in his stomach, like a thirst in his throat. When he spoke his voice had a harsh, raw-toned rasp to it. "A warning," he said.

Usher turned to Cleek. "You hear, Idaho? He's warning me. Fresh out of the calaboose and warning a respectable, law-abiding citizen. It ain't fair, Idaho. It ain't right. What shall we do about it?"

Tennant paid Cleek strict attention, knowing how this would start — if it started. Cleek's eyes continued their unblinking appraisal. He was shrewd and he was cautious. There was no pride in him, Tennant thought; no vanity. Yet Cleek showed a deliberate and thorough arrogance in the way he ignored Usher now. If Cleek took orders from Tate there was no sign of it. A stranger, Tennant reflected, would have difficulty guessing which was owner and which was foreman. And a stranger would probably guess wrong.

Cleek said flatly, "We've got no time for talk."

There was nothing formidable in the brief glance he gave Naviska, nor in the way he eased his horse a step to the left. But Tennant thought instantly, *Cleek knows the odds will never be better than they are right now,* and wondered if Cleek's milky eyes had held that same blank, unblinking stare when they'd peered at Mike Menafee over a blasting gun. They were the eyes of a man who could kill without anger, or emotion.

"So you came back for some more trouble," Cleek said, speaking with such deliberate slowness that sunlight made a steady glint on his gold teeth. "Well, you've found it, Tennant."

And Red Naviska bragged, "Trouble aplenty."

A wicked anticipation burned in Naviska's green-gray eyes; it flushed his wedge-shaped face and compressed his lips so that twin trickles of tobacco juice dribbled from the corners of his mouth. He was, Tennant thought, more dangerous in some ways than Cleek, for he had a bully's false pride and a bully's need for conflict.

"All the goddam trouble you'll ever want," Naviska added insolently.

"All Usher will ever want, also," Tennant said.

"How's that?" Usher demanded. "What you mean by that, Tennant?"

Tennant ignored him. He said to Cleek, "I

93

might not match your draw, but I'll have time for one shot at Usher, regardless. And he's too big a target for me to miss."

Cleek thought about that. His eyelids tightened perceptibly and he said, "Maybe. Maybe not."

Then, without shifting his glance from Tennant, he said, "Somebody coming east, Red. Go see who it is."

Tennant hadn't heard a sound. He was wondering how Cleek could have heard anything, when he noticed that the horses' heads were turned, ears pricked forward. Cleek had observed that instantly; all his senses were honed to the fine edge of an animal's alertness and he was sharp as a man could be. It was a good thing to know, Tennant reflected, but not a pleasant thing. Recalling how Leona had said he should be able to outsmart Usher's reedy ramrod, Tennant guessed she shared Huffmeyer's mistake of underrating Idaho Cleek.

Red Naviska gigged his horse up the road, and Usher said, "I don't like to have unfriendly neighbors, Tennant. I'll make you a price on what's left of your burned-out place."

"Here's a better proposition," Tennant offered, and kept Cleek on the fringe of his vision. "Just beat my draw right now, and Roman Four is yours."

Usher didn't like this at all. He frowned and said, "You're loco," and glanced at Cleek as if to assure himself that Cleek was fully alert.

The TU foreman sat easy in saddle, his contemplative eyes showing no change. But the position of his right hand changed so that his thumb was now hooked on the belt fold of his holster. He said flatly, "You talk real tough, jailbird."

Tennant's right hand was within four inches of his gun, and that margin of separation seemed hugely important. He had an almost overwhelming urge to move his hand closer, but he fought it down, sensing that his slightest move now would be the signal for Cleek's draw, and guessing how slim a chance he stood of matching it.

"Somebody coming," Usher said nervously.

Tennant heard the soft tinkle of a bell; he was making his own estimate of that sound when Naviska came back and reported, "Hobo Bill Wimple with his pack outfit."

"Let's get on into town," Tate Usher suggested at once. "We're way late for breakfast."

The plain note of apprehension in Usher's voice stirred a secret amusement in Tennant. Tate wasn't liking that talk about being a big target. The man was yellow to the core. . . .

Cleek said, "All right," and motioned for Usher and Naviska to go on ahead of him. Then he rode slowly past Tennant, saying, "Some other time."

"Sure," Tennant agreed.

Hobo Bill came up, riding a roan mule and driving four burros ahead of him. The lead burro wore a small, sweet-toned bell that tinkled merrily to each mincing step.

"Sure surprising who a man'll meet on a stage-road," Bill greeted, and stuck out a calloused hand. "How be you, Jeff?"

"Fine," Tennant said. He eyed Hobo Bill in friendly fashion and declared, "You don't look an hour older than that day you showed me where to find a five-pronged buck, four years ago."

Bill's leathery face showed a reflective smile. "Was it that long ago?" he asked as if genuinely surprised. "Time sure flits by a feller."

Tennant smiled, knowing that time didn't mean much to Hobo Bill who spent his summers searching for a fabulous cache of Spanish treasure supposedly hidden high on Dragoon Divide, and loafed out his winters at Mayme Shay's house. It was generally understood that Mayme had grubstaked him for years; and that their romance dated back to the hurly-burly days when Mayme had been a star performer at the Bonanza Bazaar.

This was earlier than Hobo Bill usually quit his camp on the Rim, so Tennant asked, "Did you run short of grub, or just get lonesome for the sound of Mayme's girlish laughter?"

"Neither one," Bill said, "although it'll pleasure me considerable to see Mayme again. There's a grand and glorious woman, Jeff — the finest female from here to who hid the broom!"

"Shouldn't wonder," Jeff said, observing the

bright shine that came into Bill's eyes. Bill would never be really old, Tennant guessed; he'd go on praising Mayme and hunting for hidden treasure until the day he died. . . .

"I had a good reason for leavin' the Rim early," Bill explained. He puckered his lips and expertly squirted tobacco juice between the mule's floppy ears. "It's my guess there'll be snow clean down to Tonto Flats this year. Plenty snow. All the signs point to it. Look at the coat my mule is makin', and her usually slick as a shewahwah pup at this time o' year. I'm bettin' it'll be a rip-roarin' heller of a winter."

Then he added cheerfully, "But I'll be toastin' my shins at Mayme's kitchen stove, warm as a bug in a rug."

Whereupon he kicked the mule into motion and followed his burros down the road.

Tennant sat for a moment watching Bill's departure and recalling how genial a host he had been during the two weeks his camp was used as a hunting base. No one in Bunchgrass Basin had ever accused Hobo Bill of doing a mean or dishonest thing, yet most men judged him harshly; counting him a shiftless, shameless loafer, they scoffed at his treasure hunting and considered his association with Mayme Shay a fit subject for ribald jokes. Even so, Tennant thought, some of them probably envied Bill his foot-loose freedom when he started out each spring, packing provisions to his camp on the Rim. And although it didn't occur to them that Bill cherished Mayme more than most men cherished their wives, they begrudged him his grubstake and the generous affection that went with it.

Life, Tennant reflected, was an endless riddle. By every rule in the book Bill was a pauper, yet he possessed the highest and most elusive prize of all: genuine happiness. It was enough to make a man look twice at his hole card. . . .

Tennant shrugged, and was turning the sorrel when he noticed a raveled-out plume of dust that appeared to be about a mile north of him. Someone was traveling westward in a hurry. Acting on pure impulse Tennant dismounted, climbed the rock outcrop and from this vantage point, had his look at the stageroad. There were only two riders ahead of Bill's burros now; Tennant couldn't identify them at this distance, but he was reasonably sure that Cleek wouldn't leave Usher.

"So it's Naviska," Tennant muttered, and guessing what the redhead was up to, cursed morosely. There was no adequate defense against ambush in this broken, brush-tangled country — no way a man could protect himself from a dry-gulch sneak. He tried to recall if there'd been a gun-filled scabbard on Naviska's saddle and decided there was; which meant that Red could make his play from a high bank some distance off the road.

Tennant climbed into saddle, rode westward, and wondered where Naviska would set his ambush trap. There were several likely places;

the nearest, Tennant thought, was the ford at Commissary Creek. The north bank was high, and a dry-gulcher could leave his horse well back in the mesquite thickets so there'd be no risk of a whinny revealing his presence.

Tennant considered the advisability of riding south of the road and crossing the creek west of the ford. If he rode at a walk there wouldn't be enough dust for Naviska to tally his change of route. But the redhead might not be waiting at the ford; he might choose any one of a dozen places. A man couldn't ride around them all, and there was no way of guessing which place to avoid.

Abruptly then it occurred to Tennant that there was one way of knowing exactly where Naviska's ambush would be; one sure, simple way. He thought, *Red won't be looking for me behind him. He'll be watching the stageroad all the time.*

Tennant smiled, liking this, and rode north until he came to Naviska's trail, then followed it westward without difficulty. The sign was plain, allowing him to reckon the changing speed of Red's travel by the depth and spacing of hoofprints. Presently glimpsing a discarded cigarette butt and burned match, Tennant knew Naviska had halted here long enough to smoke a cigarette. Red, he guessed, had endeavored to tally some sign of travel on the road; the TU rider was probably wondering why no dust plume showed down there.

Tennant rode slowly, stopping at frequent intervals to scan the brush-covered country ahead. There was no sign of dust now, which meant that Naviska was riding at a walk, or had already reached an ambush site that suited him. According to the direction of these horse tracks, Red was aiming for the ford at Commissary Creek.

It occurred to Tennant now that he had two choices here. He could angle north of the ford and continue his journey to Bar Bell without risk. Or he might, with a little luck, ambush an ambusher.

10. "You Mean Bare Naked?"

At noon Jeff Tennant found Naviska's bay bronc tied to a mesquite tree near the ford at Commissary Creek. The animal stood in the droopy, down-headed way of a foundered horse, his sweat-crusted flanks indicating that he'd been ridden fast and had stood here long enough to dry out. *At least half an hour,* Tennant reckoned, and noticed that the scabbard on the bay's saddle was empty.

Tennant gave the roundabout brush a questing consideration. Naviska, he guessed, was waiting with a Winchester. If the redhead had discovered he was being trailed, this would be a poor place to be caught afoot. But there was only one way to find out for sure. A man had to take his chances on a deal like this; he had to play his hunches, and hope to hell they were right. So thinking, Tennant dismounted. He tied the sorrel to a clump of cat-claw, took off his spurs and hung them on the saddle horn; then he found Naviska's boot tracks and warily followed them.

The land here was broken by a series of shallow washes running between low, rocky ridges. Tennant calculated the distance to the stageroad as being not more than an eighth of a mile, which meant that Naviska wasn't far off; he drew his gun, crossed a stone-studded wash and climbed the steep bank beyond it. Here he halted, crouching low and scanning the mesquite thickets ahead. The thought came to him that this was the first time he'd stalked a man with a gun since the Lincoln County War. He smiled, recalling how haphazardly he'd got mixed up in that affair; he had been green and gun-shy when the fighting started, but mostly he'd been afraid of being afraid. . . .

Warily, with a patient stealth that guarded against stepping on a dead branch or scuffing a stone, Tennant followed Naviska's tracks into a brush-tangled arroyo and along its crooked course for several yards before climbing out. Again he halted, and narrowly regarded the low, greasewood-fringed ridge above him. That would be the logical place for Naviska to wait; the road probably cut across its southern slope.

Now for a little luck, Tennant thought, and moved slowly up the ridge.

When he was within a few feet of the crest Tennant went to his hands and knees; he crept behind a rock outcrop and peered over it, and saw Naviska hunkered behind another outcrop directly ahead of him. Red was watching the road, and probably wondering why he'd had no target. A slow grin eased Tennant's lips. But presently, as Naviska got up and sunlight glanced off the Winchester cradled in his arms, Tennant ceased smiling. There, except for luck, stood the man who would have shot him from ambush as mercilessly as a skulking Apache. For the second time that day anger ran its swift, hot course through Jeff Tennant. He held his gun on Naviska and considered crippling him. It would be an easy thing to break Red's right arm; at this distance he could target a shirt sleeve between elbow and shoulder.

I'll teach him to play Indian, Tennant thought; he was taking deliberate aim when Naviska put down his gun and began building a cigarette. Red's right arm still made a plain target; but now, because his hands held paper and tobacco instead of a Winchester, Tennant didn't fire. There was no real difference in ethics here. The TU gunhawk was as viciously destructive as a snake at skin-shedding time; he deserved to be shot on sight, without warning or mercy, yet Tennant waited for him to pick up the gun.

As if sensing surveillance, Naviska turned abruptly. His green-gray eyes bugged wide and his tobacco-stained mouth opened and for one long moment he stared at Tennant's leveled revolver as if fascinated beyond the power to speak or move. Then he demanded, "How'd you get up here?"

"Followed snake sign," Tennant said.

Naviska still held the half-made cigarette. He brought the paper to his lips, licked its edge, tapered the brown-paper cylinder and lit it. Then he took a deep drag of smoke and asked with insolent bravado, "What in hell you figgerin' to do?"

A moment ago Tennant couldn't have told

him. But now, observing Red's attempt to play the bully, Tennant understood that pride was the prop which supported this man's viciousness. There was no cure for a dry-gulcher, save killing; but there was a way to eliminate the prop, and thus punish him. . . .

"Unbuckle that gun belt, before I do it with a bullet," Tennant ordered; and when Naviska complied, Tennant said, "Now take off your clothes."

Naviska peered at him in plain puzzlement. "What for?" he demanded.

"So you can play Apache the way it should be played," Tennant said. He motioned Naviska back, and gathered up Red's gun gear, strapping the holstered Colt so it hung on his left hip. Then he waggled his gun and said flatly, "Shuck those clothes."

"No," Naviska said sullenly. "By God, you can't make me do that!"

"Maybe not," Tennant said, and stepped close. "But I can do it for you." He raised his gun and held it as a man would hold a quirt poised for striking. He said, "You'll strip goddam easy, asleep," and slashed at Naviska's head.

Naviska dodged, evading the down-swung gun barrel, but Tennant stuck out a boot and tripped him. The redhead fell on his back and Tennant stepped astride him at once; when Naviska tried to get up, Tennant booted him back, hard enough to knock the wind out of him. Naviska's face turned pale, and a wildness burned in his round, hot eyes. He inhaled deeply, his sucked-in cheeks giving his narrow face a wolfish ferocity. But he made no further move, and Tennant asked, "Which one of us takes off your clothes, Red?"

"Me," Naviska muttered.

"Then get at it," Tennant ordered, and stepped aside.

Naviska took off his shirt. He watched Tennant pick up the rifle, and said, "I was just keepin' watch for Ben Petty, was all."

"Expecting him to come from town," Tennant scoffed. "Like hell you were."

Naviska shrugged. He stepped out of his pants and stood in sweat-stained underwear, until Tennant said impatiently, "All of it, Red."

"You mean bare naked?" Red demanded.

"Every goddam stitch," Tennant said and watched Naviska shed his underwear.

The thought came to Tennant that Naviska didn't look tough at all without his clothes. From the neck down his skin was chalk-white, except for skimpy patches of reddish hair. He looked gawky now, almost timid. Tennant grinned, knowing it was unlikely that Red would reach TU without running into one of the several riders who were searching for Ben Petty. In which case Red would never live this down. . . .

Tennant picked up Naviska's clothes and rolled them into a bundle. He said, "Now you can sneak around like a real honest-to-God Apache," and walked back across the crest.

"I'll pay you off for this, by God," Naviska called in a rage-clotted voice. "I'll pay you double!"

Tennant rummaged in the bundle of clothes and took a knife from Naviska's pants and tossed it to him, saying, "Cut yourself a bow and arrow, Red."

Naviska picked up the knife. He opened it and absently tested the sharpness of its blade with his thumb. Presently he walked to the north rim of the ridge and watched Tennant tie the bundle of clothes behind the bay bronc's saddle. Then, as Tennant rode off leading the TU bronc, Naviska cursed him in the toneless, repetitious way of a man talking to himself.

When Tennant reached the Bar Bell road he dismounted, took the bundle of clothes from Naviska's saddle and tossed it into the brush. He unbuckled Red's gun gear and sent it after the bundle. Then he turned the bay loose, reasonably sure that the animal would head for home. There was a chance that some TU rider might intercept the bay, take him in tow and subsequently find Naviska. But even so, Red would have to ride in the raw. . . .

Tennant chuckled, and jogged on toward Bar Bell. It seemed a trifle odd that he should be traveling this road. Three days ago it would have seemed fantastic. All he'd hoped for was fulfillment of an ex-convict's need for revenge. Now, if his luck held good, he had a chance to make a dream come true: to win a well-stocked spread of his own, with Jane to share it. And there would be vengeance too, of a sort, for even though Tate Usher survived the impending fight, he would be ruined if Bar Bell won.

Riding with his hat brim tilted against the sun's slanting rays, Tennant contemplated his present situation and found it good. If Ben's lawyer succeeded in exposing Usher for the scallywag he was, the fight against TU might be made less difficult in many ways. For one thing, Bar Bell would have an extra rider once Ben was freed. And there should be no interference from Sheriff Lambert after TU had been exposed as an outlaw spread. Until now Tate Usher had managed to make a show of respecting the law. His most nefarious schemes had worn a threadbare cloak of legality, and there'd been no proof that he was viciously unscrupulous. But there'd be proof aplenty if Lawyer Randall maneuvered Usher into swearing he hadn't been at Roman Four the night Ed Peebles' body was burned. Once that fact was established, and accepted by a jury, Tate Usher would be tumbled from his false throne of respectability.

Although it seemed unimportant now, Tennant recognized the chance for exoneration this deal held for him. If people believed Tate Usher had burned the body of his own rider so that Petty could be framed off his homestead, they might also believe that Usher had engineered a brand-blotting deal against another man for the same purpose. . . .

A string of horses, traveling single file, crossed the road ahead of him — a thoroughbred stallion leading seven mares and four colts toward Commissary Creek for their evening drink. This was Bar Bell's home range, rolling grassland sprawled between the Tailholt Hills on the east and Apache Peak on the west, with the towering ramparts of Dragoon Divide for a northern border. Good range, this, stocked with a better-than-average grade of cattle. If a man had his pick of all the breeder stuff in Bunchgrass Basin he would come here for his cows.

Tennant was thinking about that, and of his chance to own a share of such stock, when he rode into the Bar Bell yard at sundown. The main building was a long adobe structure with a gallery across its entire front. An ell at the north end housed the kitchen; beyond this, across the dusty yard, were a bunkhouse, a blacksmith shop and a huge wagon shed. Tennant thought, *A real cow outfit,* and understood why Leona Bell was willing to fight for its survival.

Two punchers were washing at the bucket outside the kitchen door. Tennant didn't recognize this pair, but he knew the three men who sat on a bench in front of the bunkhouse: Bravo Shafter, Pete Lunsford and Jack Ramsay.

He said, "Howdy," and rode past them to the horse corral, not liking their wordless, unsmiling appraisal. It hadn't occurred to him that Leona's crew would resent his coming here; the knowledge that they did whipped up a kindred resentment. What in hell were they sulking about? He hadn't asked for the ramrod job. This deal would be difficult enough with the full support of a loyal crew; it would be utterly hopeless with anything less.

Tennant unsaddled, turned his sorrel into the corral and hung his gear on the kak pole. Then he sauntered over to the bunkhouse and asked quietly, "Who's been repping for Huffmeyer?"

Bravo Shafter stood up. He said, "Me," and his sullen tone matched the scowl on his blocky, clean-shaved face.

"Then you're the one I've got to lick," Tennant said, and hit him.

It wasn't a hard blow; more like a shove, with Tennant's right fist striking soundlessly against Shafter's midriff. Not nearly as hard swung as the fist Bravo slammed at Tennant, and which Tennant barely dodged. But the second — a left that landed just below Shafter's right ear — was loaded; a paralyzing blow that produced results at once. Bravo's lower jaw sagged until his mouth was fully open. His big hands dropped and hung loose at his sides so that he was as wide open a target as a man could be.

"Lordy, Lordy," Jack Ramsay groaned.

And Leona, watching this from the kitchen doorway with a queerly urgent anticipation, waited wide-eyed for the final, finishing blow.

But Tennant didn't hit Shafter again. He ignored him, and walked toward the wash bench, not looking back as Bravo slumped in the slow, knee-bending fashion of a horse lying down.

The pair at the wash bench peered at Tennant in shocked silence. He picked up the bucket, and seeing Leona in the doorway, said, "Hello, boss-ma'am."

Leona smiled, and said with frank admiration, "I see you've taken charge," and then watched as he toted the bucket across the yard and doused Shafter's blank-eyed face with water.

Shakespear Smith, the bald and bearded cook who'd once tromped the boards of variety theatres, said slyly, "Methinks the lady was not jesting when she said yon lancer was tough. Like Cassius, he hath a lean and hungry look."

And at the bunkhouse old Pete Lunsford muttered, "I never seen the beat of it, him crumpling Bravo with one blow."

"He didn't learn that in no law school," Jack Ramsay said. "A man would be daft to fight that feller with his fists."

11. A Serious Offense

John Peebles, Dude Finn, Lee Pardee and Goldie Rimbaugh ate supper at Menafee Camp. Afterward, while they lounged on the front stoop, Dude Finn said, "Wonder what the hell became of Red."

"He was ridin' toward town with Tate and Idaho last I saw of him," Pardee muttered. "Them three has probably spent the day takin' their ease at Stromberg's bar."

Johnny Peebles got up and went over to the corral, whereupon Goldie Rimbaugh complained, "That kid gives me the crawlin' creeps. He's so spooky he'll be shootin' at his own shadder when the moon comes up. It ain't safe to ride within a mile of him."

They watched Johnny catch a bronc, and presently Dude said, "Funny thing we ain't seen Sheriff Sam all day. He must of stayed in town, figgerin' we'd ride our goddam pants off a-chasin' Petty for him."

"Reminds me of Lincoln County," Pardee reflected. "Chisum and Murphy was supposed to be fightin' each other, but they sat on their fat rumps while jiggers like me and Bill Bonney and Doc Skurlock rampaged around from hell to breakfast."

"Wasn't Jeff Tennant in that fracas?" Finn asked.

Pardee nodded, and glanced at Johnny Peebles. "Tennant wasn't much older'n the kid, and just about as spooky. He was a reg'lar Fancy Dan at the start, but he toughed up fast after he got shot at a few times."

Johnny Peebles called from the corral, "Ain't you fellers goin' to saddle up?"

"It'll be dark in half an hour," Finn said. "No use rimmin' around when you can't see."

And Pardee counseled, "Ain't no rush now, kid. If Petty stayed in Bunchgrass Basin we'll find him tomorrow or next day. But it's my guess he's high-tailed for the tules."

"I don't think so," Johnny muttered. "He'd of took his town suit and Sunday hat and war bag with him if he was goin' yonderly." The kid got into saddle and sat there undecided for a moment. Then he asked, "Ain't none of you goin' to ride?"

"Not me," Dude Finn declared, "I'm not missin' my shut-eye two nights runnin' for nobody."

Johnny shrugged and rode out of the yard. Ed's death, he guessed, didn't mean much to Dude and the others. Yesterday they had acted like they were all broke up over Ed being murdered; they'd talked big about catching Ben Petty and what would happen when they got hold of him. But now it didn't seem to make no never mind to them, one way or the other. All they thought about was filling their goddam gizzards and getting some shut-eye. How the hell

112

could they feel like eating or sleeping until Ben Petty was caught? Just thinking about the dirty, back-shooting sneak spoiled the taste of a man's vittles. . . .

It was fully dark when Johnny eased his horse down the slope north of Ben Petty's shack and saw yellow light bloom in the doorway. Someone had just lit a lamp. It might not mean anything, though. Cleek and the others were probably using the place to cook supper, Johnny guessed; or perhaps Sheriff Sam was taking a looksee around. But it just might be Petty, come back for some getaway provisions.

Johnny held his horse to a walk. There was no smell of smoke, no sound of talk. No broncs at the hitchrack. Anticipation grew stronger and stronger in him. By grab, it might be Petty; and if it was he could square Ed's death all by himself, without any goddam help!

The thought of it made Johnny sweat and shiver at the same time. When he came to the yard he dismounted, drew his gun, and catfooted toward the shack. Someone was in there, all right; someone who cast a long shadow when he walked between the lamp and the window. Johnny approached the shack from the west side and stepped up to the window. God, if only it were Ben Petty! . . .

Johnny peered through the dust-peppered pane. He couldn't see Petty's face, but he recognized Petty's pink-striped Sunday shirt and the blue serge pants he was pulling up. A whimpering curse slipped from Johnny's lips. He fired, saw Petty's pants slide down, and slammed two more slugs into that bent-over back.

"Just like you did it to Ed," Johnny yelled.

He climbed into saddle, and said in a surprised way, "I done it, by grab — I done it easy!"

He was riding away from the shack when Tate Usher and Idaho Cleek came galloping up and Usher asked, "What's going on?"

"Petty came back for his Sunday suit," Johnny said. He felt sort of proud about this, and added, "Just like I figgered he would."

Cleek got off his horse and went into the shack, and Usher demanded, "What you talking about?"

"I just killed Ben Petty," Johnny said.

Usher was halfway to the door. He whirled now and stared at Johnny and exclaimed, "Like hell you did — Petty is in jail!"

Then Idaho Cleek came to the doorway and announced, "It's Red Naviska, deader'n a barbecued beef."

"Red?" Johnny croaked.

"Why — you slobberin' lunatic!" Tate Usher bellowed. "You've lost me a good man!"

But Johnny wasn't listening. He ran to the doorway, peered at Red's loose-jawed face, and got sick.

Usher said to Cleek, "Red was worth ten like him and his drunken brother."

"Mebbe Red is still worth something to us,"

114

Cleek mused thoughtfully. He stepped over to Johnny and asked, "Why'd you do it, kid?"

"I thought it was Ben Petty. He was puttin' on Ben's clothes. What would Red be doin' a thing like that for?"

Cleek shook his head. "Can't figger it out," he admitted.

"That don't change things one iota," Usher declared. "Naviska is dead and this young punk killed him — shot him in the back, by God. They'll hang you for that, and it'll serve —"

Cleek broke in, saying, "Shut up, Tate."

Then he said to Johnny, "Shooting an unarmed man in the back is a serious offense, kid. You can't claim self-defense or a goddam thing."

"But I thought it was Petty," Johnny insisted.

"That wouldn't make any difference to the law," Tate Usher scoffed. "They'd say you had no right to throw three slugs into Petty's back either."

"That's how he shot Ed," Johnny muttered. "I figgered he deserved the same."

"Bad figgering," Cleek said quietly. "It'll put a rope around your neck one of these days. Now listen close, kid — and do like I tell you."

12. "Hello, Handsome!"

Bar Bell's spacious, beam-ceilinged parlor was furnished with a mahogany-and-plush elegance seldom seen so far from town. A huge fireplace rose rafter high against the south wall; in front of it a red leather lounge and two upholstered chairs were arranged to form a cozy bay beneath a crystal chandelier. Comparing this with the barrel-chair frugality of ranch houses he had known, Tennant remembered his father's pet phrase for such luxury: "Eating high on the hog."

An oil painting in a heavy gilt frame — the life-size portrait of a strikingly beautiful woman — attracted Tennant's attention as he followed Leona across the room. The picture held a flesh-and-blood aliveness, a passionate, pulsing vitality so compelling that the dark eyes seemed to sparkle and the pursed lips to part for frank smiling. There was something familiar about the picture, as if he had seen it at some other time and in some other place. He thought, *Leona resembles her,* yet when he looked at Leona there seemed to be only a slight resemblance; she had the same coloring, and somewhat similar features, but so had Rose Barlow and countless other brunettes. . . .

"I know," Leona murmured, "I suffer by contrast."

"Your mother?" Tennant asked.

116

She nodded, and Jules Huffmeyer, who'd followed them from the kitchen, said braggingly, "Mister Bell brought a famous artist all the way from Kansas City to paint that picture."

Leona motioned them to the lounge and seated herself in a chair so that she was directly facing Tennant, and asked with imperious assurance, "Why did you pick the fight with Bravo?"

Tennant considered the question, and the reason for its being asked. She had shown no displeasure immediately after the fight, nor during supper. In fact she seemed to take a secret satisfaction in it when she introduced him to Fred Eggleston and Tex Taylor, the two men he hadn't known, referring to him as the "toughest ramrod in Arizona." Yet now she demanded an explanation.

"Mebbeso that knockdown did Bravo good," Huffmeyer suggested.

"I didn't ask you," Leona said sharply, and waited for Tennant's answer.

The thought came to Tennant that there was a fiercely possessive instinct in this girl. It showed in her voice when she spoke of Bar Bell; it had been there, too, when she'd told Jules Huffmeyer that he would do no riding until his ribs were properly knitted. She had, he guessed, taken possession of Huffmeyer's loyalty and transformed it into obedience. He wondered if she was expecting to reshape her new ramrod to the same pattern and by the same process, first gaining his loyalty, then using it as a club to force obedience.

So thinking, Tennant asked, "Am I supposed to explain my actions every time I do something around here?"

Swift resentment brightened Leona's eyes and deepened the color of her cheeks. Tennant watched its warming effect; he looked at the picture again and understood why it had seemed familiar. Leona closely resembled her mother now. . . .

"Is there any good reason why you shouldn't tell me?" she demanded.

"None at all," Tennant admitted. He glanced at Huffmeyer, and caught an expression of puzzlement in the old man's faded eyes; then he said to Leona, "My reason for hitting Bravo was pretty obvious. You know why I did it, but you want to hear me offer an excuse. Well, I'm not in the habit of giving excuses for what I do."

For a dozen seconds, while Huffmeyer sat straight as a buggy whip and watched with hushed expectancy, these two strong-willed people eyed each other in unwavering appraisal — until Leona shrugged and said, "No, I guess not."

She smiled thinly and added, "Perhaps that's one of the reasons why I wanted to hire you."

The clatter of Shakespear Smith's dish washing came from the kitchen; and presently the plaintive twang of a banjo drifted across from the bunkhouse. Tennant put his fingers to shaping a cigarette. "What are you planning to do about those steers on Tonto Flats?" he inquired casually.

"I want them rounded up and driven to the Rio Pago. I'd like to see them pushed right into Usher's front yard."

"And supposin' TU starts shootin' while it's bein' done?" Jules asked.

"We'll shoot back at them, and shoot to kill," Leona declared. "Every TU rider knocked out of saddle is one less we'll have to fight."

Tennant marveled at this girl's seeming eagerness to plunge her crew into a shooting war. He wondered if she had ever seen a rider knocked from saddle by a bullet, or heard a gut-shot man moan out his agony, or seen broncs drift home at dawn with blood-smeared saddles. . . .

She said, "I happen to know that Usher is in no shape to hire more gun-slingers. He's going to be real short of cash until he delivers those steers to the Indian Agency. I wish there were some way to drive them so far Usher couldn't gather them in time to fill his contract next January. That would save my winter feed and put Usher over a barrel to boot. But I don't suppose it's possible."

"With a little luck," Tennant said, "anything is possible."

He got up and selected a chunk from the stacked wood beside the fireplace and put it across the andirons.

"It'd take luck aplenty to hide three hundred steers where TU couldn't find 'em," Huffmeyer muttered.

"I know a place they'd be lost for months,"

Tennant said, "if we could figure a way to get a day's head start."

"One day?" Leona asked. "Only one day's start?"

Tennant nodded. "Usher probably won't bother us much more while we round up and cut out Bar Bell stuff. It's my guess he'll wait for us to drive his steers past Menafee Camp before he makes a move. That way he can claim he was within his legal rights and didn't jump us until we trespassed on his range."

"More'n likely," Huffmeyer agreed. "He's slicker'n cow slobbers."

"Well," Tennant said, "suppose instead of driving those steers toward the Rio Pago we hustle them across Bar Bell range to the Slot. If we could get them halfway to Spanish Pass before Usher knew what we were up to, all hell couldn't stop us. There's no way a horse can climb the divide except by the Slot Trail. Once Usher's steers are strung out and climbing, a rear guard of two men could hold off an army."

Leona had been frowningly attentive. Now she smiled and eyed Tennant with frank admiration. "If the steers were pushed through Spanish Pass and down the other side they'd scatter in that Crazy Canyon country," she said excitedly. "It would take Usher's crew a couple of months to gather them again."

Even Jules Huffmeyer seemed to be impressed and said, "By that time there'd be ten-foot drifts in Spanish Pass."

"Yeah," Tennant mused. "I met Hobo Bill today and he says we're going to have an early winter."

Leona got up and smacked the palm of her left hand with a tight-clenched fist and exclaimed, "Jeff — you've hit it!"

She paced back and forth in front of the fireplace. "We've got to figure a way to do it," she insisted. "We've got to!"

"A decoy herd might do it," Tennant suggested. "Drive Bar Bell stuff toward the Rio Pago while TU steers start west. If we did it at night Usher'd have no way of knowing the Bar Bell herd was a decoy. He'd think it was his own stuff being driven off our range."

"That's it!" Huffmeyer said at once. "That'll git the job done!"

"And it will break Tate Usher," Leona reflected happily. "He'll lose out on the Agency contract and be so short of cash his crew will quit him."

"The plan isn't foolproof," Tennant cautioned. "A lot can happen between now and the night we start a decoy herd north. But it's worth a try."

He turned to Huffmeyer and asked, "How long will it take to gather a *remuda?*"

"There's upward of twenty broncs in the horse trap right now," Jules reported. "All broke and ready to work. Tex Taylor could haze 'em into the corral before breakfast — if you want to start your roundup tomorrow."

121

"I see no reason why we shouldn't," Tennant said and looked to Leona for possible objections. He got none.

Then he said, "It's going to take considerable riding to chouse those steers out of the brush." He glanced at Leona, and added, "I'll need your cook, which means you and Jules will have to rustle your own grub for a spell."

Without waiting for acceptance of this decision, Tennant went to the kitchen and inquired, "How are you fixed for supplies, Shakespear?"

"We possess an abundance of plain but nourishing food," the cook assured him with a theatrical flourish of his hands. "I would hesitate to call this kitchen a cornucopia due to a slight deficiency of fresh fruit, but otherwise it is a veritable horn of plenty."

Tennant said, "Good," and went on to the doorway. "You'll be taking the chuck wagon to Tonto Flats in the morning."

"Lord God of hosts!" Smith exclaimed.

Sheriff Sam Lambert was playing cribbage with Doc Medwick when Johnny Peebles stepped into the jail office and announced, "I got more bad news, Sheriff."

"What now?" Lambert asked disgustedly and threw down his cards. "Somebody else been murdered?"

Johnny nodded.

"Who?" Lambert demanded.

"Red Naviska. He was shot in the back."

"Who done it?" Lambert asked.

"Jeff Tennant," Johnny said. He cuffed trail dust from his shirt and glanced at the dim-lit corridor which led to the cells. "I didn't exactly see it happen, though."

"Then how do you know Jeff did it?" Doc Medwick inquired.

"Well, I was rimmin' around near Petty's place along about sundown. I heard three shots and saw Tennant whirl away from a window and ride off, hell-bent. Then I went to the shack and found Red layin' face down on the floor. He was dead."

"Sufferin' saints!" Lambert blurted. He peered at Doc and exclaimed accusingly, "So Tennant is just a tough-talkin' galoot, eh? He's been back three days and two men are murdered. By God, I wouldn't be surprised if it was him that killed Ed Peebles!"

Doc Medwick shrugged. He get up and said wearily, "I suppose we've got to go out there tonight. This coroner job is getting to be a tedious chore."

Then he asked Johnny, "Are you sure it was Tennant you saw?"

"Positive," Johnny insisted. "I got a good look at his face."

"Then why the hell didn't you take a shot at him?" Lambert asked.

"I didn't know what had happened till I looked into the shack. Then it was too late."

Lambert took his hat from the wall peg.

"Usher has lost two men in three days' time," he muttered. "Tate'll be downright pestilential about this."

"You want to ride with me in the buggy?" Doc Medwick asked.

"Might as well. No tellin' where Tennant is by now. He might be camped somewhere near his burnt-out shack, but I ain't relishin' the chore of lookin' for him at night. You know what, Doc — I think them three years at Yuma has turned him loco. I think he's gone kill-crazy!"

"Might be," Doc admitted. But even so he didn't mention the fact that Tennant could probably be found at Bar Bell. . . .

Lambert said to Johnny, "You stay in town, son. I'll want a signed statement from you in the morning."

"Yes, sir," Johnny agreed, and went to the Palace Saloon and ordered a drink.

"What you sweatin' about?" Sid Stromberg inquired.

Instead of answering, Johnny stared at Stromberg's swollen nose and bandaged hand. "Who did that to you, Sid?"

"None of your goddam business," Stromberg said crankily.

There wasn't anyone else in the saloon and presently Stromberg said, "Don't dawdle all night with that drink. I'm closing up."

"You sure ain't very sociable," Johnny complained. He downed the whiskey and ordered another, and grimaced when he drank it. He had never taken two drinks in such rapid succession; he wondered if they'd make him drunk, and hoped they would.

"Is that all?" Stromberg asked impatiently.

Johnny nodded and went out to the stoop.

Except for the livery's high-hung lantern and a bloom of lamplight at the hotel doorway, Main Street was dark. A cold breeze came out of the north, bringing a smell of winter. Johnny shivered, and watched Doc's rig leave the livery, and wondered if Jeff Tennant's gun used the same size bullets as his. Those .45-caliber slugs sure messed a man up at close range. Idaho had said not to worry about it. But a feller couldn't help thinking, especially when he was alone. Maybe if he had somebody to talk to.

Stromberg barred the saloon door from the inside and put out the lamps. Johnny felt more alone than ever, then, standing on the dark stoop. He walked slowly down a side street to Sashay Alley and followed it to Mayme Shay's house. When he opened the front door a bell jangled somewhere back in the house; then a blond-haired girl in a blue silk kimono came downstairs and said smilingly, "Hello, handsome."

13. Fugitive

A thin mantle of frost silvered the ground when Tennant helped Tex Taylor and Fred Eggleston haze twenty broncs out of the Bar Bell yard. There was a brief mix-up at the front gate — sharp rebel yells and a flurry of fast riding to turn a trio of bunch-quitters; then, as the saddle band settled into an orderly procession along the road, Tennant jogged back to the chuck wagon where Bravo Shafter and Jack Ramsay were loading tarp-covered bedrolls.

Dismounting beside Bravo, Tennant asked, "How far east will we find TU steers?"

Shafter had maintained a sullen silence at the breakfast table and seemed reluctant to talk now. He heaved the last bedroll up to Ramsay, not glancing at Tennant. "Ain't seen none east of Smoke Arroyo," he said finally. "The graze sort of peters out down that way."

Tennant stood silent for a moment, considering the tone of Bravo's voice, not quite sure that it was civil. According to Leona, who stood now in the kitchen doorway with Jules Huffmeyer, Bravo was the best all-round man on the crew and Tennant disliked the idea of firing him. Bar Bell was short handed as it was, yet Bravo might well become a troublemaker. . . .

"Smoke Arroyo," Tennant mused, recalling the location of that landmark and its surroundings. Then he went over to the barn where Shakespear Smith was untangling a snarled harness.

"Here," the cook proclaimed dismally, "is irrefutable proof that careless haste makes shameful waste."

"There's no rush, just so you get to Soldier Spring in time to cook supper," Tennant told him, and stepped aside as Pete Lunsford came up leading four mules.

This was a full hour after daylight, yet it was cold enough to make smoky puffs of the mules' breaths and Lunsford had to turn up the collar of his mackinaw. When Tennant walked to his ground-hitched horse he peered thoughtfully at the massed clouds above Dragoon Divide and remembered Hobo Bill's prediction. The early snow part of it, he guessed, was going to be fulfilled. There was a smell of winter in the air this sunless morning. . . .

Shafter and Ramsay were already mounted. Tennant stepped into saddle and waited until Lunsford joined them. Then he said, "Let's ride."

They were passing the house when Leona ran out and handed a blue bottle of pills to old Pete, and said censuringly, "I think you forgot them on purpose."

Then she turned to Tennant, smiling up at him and saying, "Good luck, Jeff."

Her voice was soft, almost intimate; there was a hint of emotion in it, and in the warm brightness of her eyes. She was, Tennant decided, a complex and thoroughly unpredictable girl. He said, "Thank you, ma'am," and was wondering about the look in her eyes when he led the crew out of the yard.

Presently, as they overtook the *remuda,* Tennant fell in beside Shafter and said, "Shakespear will make camp at Soldier Spring. We'll use the flats there for a holding ground until we've worked the east end clean of cattle."

"Good idea," Bravo said civilly.

He dug a Durham sack from inside his mackinaw and offered it to Tennant. "Smoke?"

Tennant nodded, showing no sign of the satisfaction that rose swiftly in him. Until this moment there'd been some doubt in his mind about the wisdom of keeping Bravo on the pay roll. One resentful rider could spoil the unity of a crew, and unity was the prime essential in time of trouble. But there was no doubt now. . . .

Jack Ramsay dropped back beside Tennant and asked, "You reckon Usher's bunch will give us any trouble while we're makin' our gather?"

"No," Tennant said, liking the friendly tone of this lanky rider's voice. "Don't believe they'll bother us for the first few days."

Pete Lunsford grunted agreement. "Not until we git up into the Tailholts," he prophesied. "Then it'll be Katey bar the door."

Tennant hadn't revealed his full plan to the crew and saw no reason to do so now. They believed that the impending drive of TU steers was

128

to be toward the Rio Pago, which was the logical destination, and so they'd make no unintentional slips if TU riders engaged them in conversation.

Sunlight broke through a rift in the overcast, gilding the steepled crests of the Twin Sombreros and slanting across the weather-carved castles of Dragoon Divide. "El Sol," Pete Lunsford drawled smilingly and turned down his collar. "An old man's best friend."

They came to the Bar Bell fork in the road and the crew were about to follow the *remuda* cross country when Tennant heard the hoof pound of a running horse. He halted at once and, during the brief interval of waiting, wondered who the oncoming rider might be. Someone from town, and in a hell of a hurry. . . .

The idea that it might be Ben Petty occurred to Tennant; but he thought, *That jigger wouldn't break jail if they left the door wide open.*

"It sounds," Bravo suggested, "like bad news traveling fast."

Then Joe Barlow galloped up on a sweat-stained livery bronc and announced excitedly, "Jeff — they're comin' after you!"

"Who?" Tennant asked, eyeing Barlow sharply and wondering if he was drunk this early in the morning.

"The whole TU bunch is in town and Sheriff Sam has sworn 'em in as deputies. You was seen at Petty's cabin yesterday afternoon."

That didn't make sense to Tennant. "What of

it?" he demanded.

Joe Barlow nudged back his battered Stetson. His glance shifted to the three Bar Bell riders behind Tennant; then he asked, "You want them to hear it?"

Tennant nodded.

Whereupon Joe said, "Well, Red Naviska was killed at Petty's place — shot three times in the back. They brung his body in late last night. He was wearin' Ben's shirt and pants."

"So," Tennant mused.

He thought about this in frowning silence for a moment, knowing why Naviska had gone to Petty's cabin for clothes — and guessing how he'd happened to get shot. Someone had mistaken Red for Ben. . . .

He asked, "Who saw me at Petty's shack?"

"Young Johnny Peebles. He says you was lookin' in a window just after he heard some shots. He says you killed Naviska."

Tennant thought instantly, *The kid shot Red by mistake, and I'm to be the goat!* This, he understood, was another slick-rigged deal like the brand-blotting, and the burning of Ed Peebles' body. It seemed ironical that he should be accused of killing Naviska after passing up a perfect opportunity to cripple the redhead yesterday. Trouble, Tennant reflected, had a way of tagging a man, and trapping him when he least expected it. A few moments ago he had been free to ride as he chose; now, by the simple process of hearing Barlow's warning, he was a fugitive from justice. Without firing a shot he had acquired the hide-out role so willingly relinquished by Ben Petty.

He asked, "Did you hear Lambert say anything about me being at Bar Bell?"

"Nope — Sam seemed to think you'd be camped at Roman Four, which was where I was headin' to," Barlow said.

That, Tennant decided, must mean that Doc Medwick hadn't told about him taking the ramrod job. He grinned and said, "Thanks for getting the word to me so fast, Joe."

"Wasn't no bother," Barlow said. "Anythin' else I can give you a hand with, Jeff?"

Tennant shook his head. "Reckon you'd better ride north of the road on your way back to town, so you won't run into the posse."

Then, noticing that Barlow's horse had left plain tracks in the road's deep dust, another idea came to Tennant. Sheriff Lambert would be sure to see that sign and wonder who had preceded him; the old lawman might detail a rider to follow Joe's tracks back to town. But if Joe rode east now with the crew, and there was a set of tracks continuing north. . . .

Tennant said, "I wish you'd go along with these Bar Bell boys for a ways, Joe, so you won't leave a trail for the posse to follow."

"Suits me fine," Joe agreed and eased his horse over to where Pete Lunsford waited. "Long time no see, Pete. You ain't hit town for a month or more."

"Been feelin' poorly," Lunsford reported. "Mebbe I'm gittin' old."

Tennant peered eastward, watching for some sign of travel and guessing the dust was too damp to raise a banner. He turned to Bravo and said, "You take charge of the work while I do a little posse-dodging. Lambert may not know I went to work for Bar Bell. It'll make things simpler all around if no one tells him."

"Sure," Shafter agreed. "We ain't even seen you."

Jack Ramsay drawled, "We'll tell old Shakespear to keep your vittles warm in case you should need some supper after dark tonight."

They rode off then, Barlow with them, and Tennant heard Bravo say, "Naviska was always lookin' for gun trouble. I'm pleasured he found it with Jeff instead of me."

A cynical smile quirked Tennant's lips as he put his horse over the place where the crew had crossed. Six riders and twenty loose broncs had come down the Bar Bell road; if Lambert took time to sort out the tracks he would discover that the same number had gone on through the brush. Tennant lifted his horse to a lope. No telling how soon the posse would be coming along, and there were a couple of chores that needed doing. When he came to Menafee Camp he hurriedly unsaddled the Bar Bell bronc he was riding and turned it loose. There were two horses in the corral; he roped a gray, and then, discovering that it had been badly gored, saddled a short-coupled grulla.

When he angled into the brush ten minutes later Tennant hazed the gray ahead of him.

14. Cold Wind Blowing

It was well after noon when Tennant approached Usher's headquarters ranch — a square log house surrounded by shacks, sheds and corrals. A single ribbon of smoke rose from a stovepipe atop the long, low-roofed cookshack; except for that, and several broncs in the horse corral, there was no sign of life.

Nobody home but the cook, Tennant thought, and turned in saddle to peer at his back trail. The sun, which had alternately shone and hidden behind shifting cloud banks, was out now; but there was no warmth in it. And no sign of travel on the flats, nor on the near slopes of the Tailholts. The posse, Tennant reckoned, was too far back to interrupt this play — in which case his plan should be fool-proof. The grulla bronc he was riding wore Usher's brand, and the cook wouldn't be expecting Jeff Tennant to pay a visit here. . . .

When he rode into the yard Tennant noticed numerous small skeletons among the scatteration of tin cans and rubbish. At first he guessed the bleached bones were those of coyotes, but when he saw others between the house and corrals it occurred to him that coyotes wouldn't make targets of themselves by coming into the yard.

"Must be dogs," Tennant decided, and pres-

134

ently, as he neared the cookshack, he was greeted by barking, penned-up dogs.

Riding close to the pens, Tennant saw an assortment ranging from suckling pups to full-grown dogs. Why, he wondered, would Tate Usher keep so many? And why were they penned up?

A bald-headed oldster wearing a flour-sack apron stood in the doorway. He called, "Howdy, stranger — light down and rest your saddle."

"*Gracias*," Tennant said, and dismounted. Nodding at the dog pens, he asked, "Why all the canines?"

"Cleek uses 'em for target practice," the cook explained, and seemed genuinely pleased to have company. "Idaho turns a few loose at a time and shoots at 'em afoot and horseback, so's to keep his hand in. Won't let nobody else shoot 'em — not even Usher."

"So," Tennant mused, understanding how Cleek maintained his speed and accuracy with a gun. "Does he hold target practice often?"

"Almost every day, except when he runs short of males, like now. It's sure a sight to see him work on them dogs. He'll come out of his office, mebbe talkin' to somebody, or saddlin' his horse, when a dog trots past; then he'll draw so damn fast you can't see it and slam two-three slugs into that dog."

The cook glanced at the grulla's brand. "You hired out with Usher?" he inquired.

Tennant nodded and said, "Last night, in town."

"They call me Baldy," the cook announced expectantly.

But Tennant ignored this invitation to tell his name. "Cleek and the others are helping the sheriff look for a galoot they say needs hanging," he explained. "I'm supposed to load a pack horse with provisions for them, so they won't have to waste time coming in for grub and ammunition."

Then he added casually, "Cleek said you'd know which horse to pack."

"Sure," Baldy agreed. "That jug-headed old bay with the blazed face and black points. You'll find a packsaddle hangin' in the wagon shed."

Tennant took down his catch rope and walked over to the corral. This, he reflected, was going even better than he'd hoped. Bachelor-camp cooks were cranky and unsociable as a rule; but Baldy seemed eager to cooperate, for he crossed the yard and unlocked the door of a building which Tennant guessed was the commissary.

The bay was easy to catch. Tennant led him from the corral and purposely left the gate open. If the cook didn't notice this there'd be no fresh mounts awaiting Usher's crew. Tennant cinched up the packsaddle and went over to the commissary stoop where canned goods, bacon, flour, coffee and boxed cartridges awaited him.

"Better give me a skillet or two," Tennant suggested. "Also a few potatoes, so we won't get scurvy."

It was a matter of minutes then until the provisions were securely packed aboard the bay and Tennant gave Baldy a farewell salute. *He'll hate me for this as long as he lives,* Tennant thought, and regretted the necessity of tricking so cheerful a man. But bounteous provisions removed the need of calling at Bar Bell or the roundup camp for food. A man could hide out indefinitely this way; he could choose his camping places and change them often enough to confuse a posse.

That had been Tennant's plan, but now a new strategy came to him. Cleek, he supposed, would put Bar Bell and the roundup camp under strict surveillance, believing them logical traps to lure a hungry fugitive. But when Usher's ramrod learned about this raid on TU's commissary he might change his tactics. . . .

Once Cleek knows I'm supplied with food he'll pull his whole crew into the hills to hunt my hide-out, Tennant thought. He considered this new angle, liking it more and more. If Cleek quit watching the roundup camp there'd be a chance to give Bar Bell's crew a hand with the gather — and to keep in touch with town.

A gray barricade of clouds converging from the north and west had blotted out the sun when Tennant reached the Rio Pago. Glancing back at TU he saw the cook rush toward the corral as horses began galloping across the yard. Thoroughly satisfied, Tennant rode into shallow water and splashed westward for a good three miles before leaving the river.

★ ★ ★

Idaho Cleek and Tate Usher reached Menafee Camp at two o'clock. They had followed a single set of hoofprints and now, as Cleek read sign, he said, "Somebody changed horses and turned the others loose."

"Who the hell would do that?" Usher demanded. "It couldn't be Tennant, because we followed these tracks all the way from town."

"Is there any reason why Tennant couldn't of spent the night in town?" Cleek asked sarcastically.

"No, there ain't," Usher admitted. He peered about the clearing as if fearful of attack, and asked, "Do you reckon it's Tennant we're trailing?"

Cleek nodded. He followed the tracks into the brush and presently, noticing how far back Usher lagged, called, "No need to be afraid of jumping him around here. This sign is a couple hours old."

"Don't be so damned sharp with your tongue," Usher complained. "I don't like it."

Cleek loosed a derisive cackle. "Mebbe you'd like to fire me," he suggested, "on account of my tongue bein' so sharp."

Usher made no reply. But there was a flare of impotent rage in his pouched eyes as he followed his reedy foreman. Cleek always got mean when there was trouble; he was like a lobo smelling raw meat . . .

Later, when the trail turned toward TU, Cleek

muttered, "It's Tennant, and I got a hunch what the smart-alecky son is up to."

It was almost dark when they rode into the ranch yard and listened to Baldy's report of a visitor. "Didn't give his name. Just said he'd been sent to get provisions so's —"

"You stinking old half-wit!" Usher exclaimed. "You've grubstaked Jeff Tennant!"

He shook a fist at Baldy and bellowed, "You're fired!"

"Leave him alone," Cleek ordered, "unless you want to do the cookin' around here."

Then, as Usher tromped off toward the corral, Cleek said, "Fix us up a bait of grub, Baldy, while we saddle fresh horses."

"Sure," the cook agreed, and turned toward the stove. Then he said dejectedly, "There ain't no fresh horses. Tennant left the corral gate open and they all run off."

Cleek cursed. His right hand slid to holster and his eyes took on the squint Baldy had seen so many times when Idaho shot at dogs. But Cleek didn't draw, and so the cook put his trembling hands to preparing supper.

Ten miles northwest of TU Jeff Tennant was also preparing supper. A cold wind came off the Dragoons; it whipped up swirls of dust in the arroyo where Tennant camped, and it brought a plain smell of moisture.

"Raining up on the rim right now," Tennant reflected. "Or maybe snowing."

Either rain or snow would make this posse-dodging deal a dismal proposition. But now the fine smell of sizzling bacon, combined with coffee coming to a boil, whetted his appetite. He flipped a skillet of fried potatoes with practiced ease and his flame-lit face held a cheerful grin as he thought, *This meal is on Tate Usher.*

After eating his fill, Tennant busied himself gathering firewood. "Going to be a long cold night," he predicted. "And maybe a wet one."

When he had a good supply of mesquite gathered, Tennant climbed part way up the rocky arroyo with a gunny sack of provisions and made a cache by dropping it between two huge boulders and covering it with stones. Then, backing down the bank, he brushed out his boot tracks with a mesquite branch.

Making his plans for the morrow, Tennant chose a place for another cache — in Bent Elbow Canyon, near the foot of the Slot Trail. After that he would turn the pack horse loose and head for Bar Bell while the posse tried to find his hideout . . .

Hunkered close to the small fire, Tennant listened to the methodical munching of his hobbled horses, browsing near by. This, he reflected, was the way it had been during the Lincoln County War: lonely campfires and dismal dawns. He wondered about Jane's reaction to the charge that he had killed Red Naviska. Would she believe Kid Peebles' story of cold-blooded murder?

Joe Barlow had seemed to believe it. So had the Bar Bell crew. It wouldn't make any difference to them, nor to Leona, who'd said the fight could be won by using the dirty, underhanded tricks Usher used. But murder would make a difference to Jane, if she believed Peebles' story. There was no doubt in Tennant's mind on that score. None at all. Jane could overlook impulsive violence in a man, and could balance his bitterness against what she called becoming a hired gun-slinger. But she would never countenance murder, nor associate with a man she thought was capable of it.

"She'd shrink every time I came near her," Tennant muttered, and the certainty of it was like a cold wind blowing. . . .

15. Stallion Bait

At seven o'clock Dude Finn dismounted on a low hill directly north of the Bar Bell yard and stamped his feet to get the chill out of them. He had replaced Goldie Rimbaugh here at six, with orders to remain until relieved at midnight.

"Not a sign of Tennant," Rimbaugh had reported. "Just old Jules and the girl, near as I can make out."

Now, instead of riding circle around Bar Bell, Dude walked, leading his horse. A man could get tolerable cold riding slow, especially when he was in sight of cheerful, lamplit windows.

"Hell of a way to earn a livin'," Dude muttered.

Afterward, as he trudged around the big yard, he got to thinking how he'd like to be spending the night in town. It would be nice and warm in the hotel dining room, with Rose Barlow smiling at him as she served supper. Just thinking about Rose warmed Dude's blood. She was a teaser if ever he'd seen one. . . .

Dude was on the kitchen side of the house now, near enough to catch a glimpse of Leona Bell when she passed a window. There, he thought, was another girl who could keep a man warm on a chilly night. She looked a lot like Rose Barlow, only she had more class to her — more style and uppity pride. But underneath she was no different from Rose, or any other girl.

He made another circle of the yard, and presently, when wind-driven rain came slanting out of the north, Dude cursed himself for failing to tie a slicker behind his saddle. Again he came to the kitchen side of the house. But instead of standing at a distance, he moved in until the building partially shielded him from wind and rain. Standing close to the wall he peered through the window and watched Leona tote dishes from table to sink. She wore a red blouse and a skirt that fitted snugly across her trim hips.

She even walks proud, Dude thought. He built a cigarette, taking care to cup his hands so the match flare wouldn't show. He smoked the cigarette down and watched the window, wanting another glimpse of Leona. He remembered a schoolteacher in Texas who'd seemed so uppity she would scream if a man so much as laid a hand on her — and recalled how willingly she'd let him kiss her. Maybe this Leona girl was the same way, Dude reflected, and he tantalized himself imagining how it would be to have her in his arms.

He tied his horse to a stoop post and was turning toward the window when Leona opened the kitchen door and asked, "What do you want?"

The abruptness of it startled Finn. He guessed she must've seen his cigarette. He said, "Why, I was wanting to get out of the rain, ma'am. It's tol'able wet and cold out here."

"Then you better come into the kitchen," she invited. "I suppose you're watching for Jeff Tennant."

Dude nodded, so surprised by her invitation that he was momentarily speechless. He followed her into the kitchen and took up a position in front of the stove, holding his palms to its welcome warmth and watching Leona pour a cup of coffee.

"Have you had supper?" she asked, and when he nodded, she said, "Here's a cup of coffee to thaw you out," and placed it on the table.

Remembering his manners, Dude took off his hat and said, "Thank you, ma'am." This, he told himself, was like that time in Texas when he'd called on the schoolteacher. Only it was better, for that one hadn't been half so good looking. Covertly watching Leona as she washed the dishes, Dude decided she was the prettiest girl he'd ever known. And the classiest. . . .

"What makes you think Jeff Tennant would come here?" Leona inquired.

Dude grinned and said apologetically, "It ain't my idea, ma'am. Idaho Cleek seems to figger Tennant will git hungry and either come here or to the roundup camp for vittles. Idaho has got men watching both places, also them homesteaders east of the Pot Holes and the road to town. In fact there's guards everywhere, except at TU."

"Then that's probably where Tennant will go to eat," Leona suggested. She smiled at Finn and asked slyly, "Do you think Tennant would take a job if I offered him one?"

Dude shook his head. "Your daddy helped send him to jail. They say Tennant came back to square up with everybody who was on the jury that convicted him. He half killed Sid Stromberg with his fists, and tried to talk Usher into a shoot out. He's got a loco streak in him, ma'am. Look how he murdered Red Naviska — not givin' Red a chance."

"Then," Leona said thoughtfully, "perhaps it's a good thing you are here. I'd hate to have Tennant take out his spite on me."

Dude nodded agreement, liking the idea that this girl considered him as a protector even though there was bad feeling between Bar Bell and TU. It might make it easier to get around her pride. . . .

He gulped down the last of his coffee and joined her at the sink, saying, "Let me wipe 'em for you, ma'am."

Leona smiled. "That's real nice of you," she said softly and handed him a towel in such a manner that their hands made brief contact. She met his gaze directly, seeing a swift rise of desire bring boldness to his eyes. A knowing smile creased his nearly-handsome, cleft-chinned face, and all his masculine vanity was in that smile.

Jules Huffmeyer came in from the living room. He stared at Finn and exclaimed, "What in hell you doin' here?"

"He's helping me with the dishes," Leona explained, "and he may help me in another way, later on."

"Such as what?" Huffmeyer demanded, thoroughly baffled.

Leona looked at Finn, forcing an intimacy in the smile she showed him before shifting her gaze to Huffmeyer. "Dude may decide he wants to be on the winning side. He may let us know the exact time Usher plans to jump my crew when they drive those TU steers toward the Rio Pago."

"But I thought —" Huffmeyer said impulsively. Then the old foreman shook his head. "It — well, I reckon mebbe you're right," he finished lamely and turned back into the living room.

Finn eyed Leona wonderingly. "You reckon there's a chance of Bar Bell winnin' out against TU?"

"Of course we'll win," Leona assured him. "I've arranged to hire more men, in Tucson and El Paso. It will take a little time for them to get here, but when they do we'll make short work of Usher's ragtag bunch."

Then she lifted a hand quickly to her mouth and exclaimed, "I shouldn't have told you that, Dude. I forgot you're still on Usher's pay roll."

The use of his first name stirred a studhorse boldness in Finn. He put down the towel and took Leona by the shoulders and said gustily,

"I'll be on your pay roll too, if you like, honey. And it won't take much to pay me."

He took his kiss then, ignoring the pressure of her resisting hands.

16. "You're My Kind of Man"

For two days and nights, while snow silvered the high Dragoons, Jeff Tennant played a crafty game of hide and seek with the TU posse. Making no effort to break through toward town, he drew Usher's riders deep into the roughs around Bent Elbow Canyon and made life miserable for them. By day he circled until he cut fresh tracks, then followed a pair of riders who were also tracking him — hour after hour. At night he built false campfires, remaining only long enough to get one well started before riding off to build another. And on two successive nights he interrupted the posse's supper by crashing through brush near their campfire and enticing them into futile pursuit.

Then, with a cold rain drenching the Tailholt Hills on the third day, Tennant changed his tactics. Deliberately allowing himself to be seen, he started up the Slot Trail so late in the afternoon that it was dark by the time he reached the first steep switchback turn. Here he halted, listened for sound of pursuit, and heard none.

Afraid of ambush, he thought; *they'll guard the Slot and wait for daylight.*

Water rushing down the deep-grooved trail was already washing out his tracks. He wondered if the posse would ride up to Hobo Bill's camp on the rim tomorrow, and hoped it would.

"That'd give me a couple free days," Tennant mused.

Whereupon he angled along the boulder-strewn slope for another mile, then made a cautious descent and rode toward Bar Bell.

This, Tennant reflected, marked the end of his fun. Usher's bunch might scout the rim, or even take a looksee into the Crazy Canyon country, believing him to be there. That meant three or four days of grace at the most. And because snow was already falling in Spanish Pass the roundup had to be completed within a week, or the drifts might be too deep. . . .

He was thinking about that, and endeavoring to calculate the time it would take to finish the gather, when he rode into the Bar Bell yard. Leona came to the kitchen door at once, calling, "Come have a cup of coffee," and adding a name that sounded like Dude.

Tennant wondered about that. He said, "I'll take more than coffee," and grinned as Leona exclaimed, "Why, Jeff — I didn't recognize you!"

Afterward, when he'd taken care of his horse and sat down to a plate piled high with warmed-up beef and potatoes, he asked, "How's the roundup coming?"

"They moved camp yesterday," Leona reported. "They're working the north flats."

"Making better time than I expected. Didn't figure five riders could clean out the east end in so short a time," Tennant said.

Leona smiled, saying, "The crew has grown

149

since you left. Joe Barlow and young Billy are on the pay roll."

Seeing his frown, she asked, "What's the matter, Jeff?"

Tennant shrugged. He said, "I promised Joe's wife I wouldn't let him side me."

"But he's not, Jeff — he's simply working for wages and I'm paying them. Not you."

Then she said, "I've got more news. Ben Petty is out of jail. Not only that, he left Bunchgrass Basin and took Rose Barlow with him."

That news astonished Tennant. "How?" he asked. "How'd Ben get out of jail?"

"A way you'd never guess," she told him. "A way so slick that only Tate Usher would think of it."

Tennant waited, aware now that she was purposely whetting his curiosity. A mischievous smile dimpled her cheeks; that, and the half-parted, pouty curve of her lips, reminded him of Rose Barlow. . . .

"Give up?" she asked.

Tennant nodded.

"Well, it seems that Usher visited Ben and offered to put up a thousand-dollar bail if Ben would leave the country. I suppose Ben was half crazy with being penned in a cell, and afraid a jury might convict him. Anyway, Usher put up the bail and Ben caught the next stage east — along with the Barlow girl."

Then she asked, "Who do you suppose told me all this?"

Tennant shrugged, not caring. He said, "So Usher gets Petty's homestead for one thousand dollars, and spoils my ace in the hole. The ace that would've proved he framed me three years ago."

But that didn't seem to impress Leona at all. She said, "You'd never guess who told me, Jeff."

Tennant shook his head. Leona, he thought, was in high spirits tonight. There was a glow in her eyes and a plain note of triumphant satisfaction in her voice when she said, "Dude Finn gave me the news — and he'll be giving me more, from time to time. Important news."

She told him then about Dude's first visit; how the TU rider had snapped at her bait. "The plan came to me the moment I saw him out there," she said. "He thinks he's irresistible to women."

"So you made him sure of it by letting him kiss you," Tennant mused.

Leona blushed. "I didn't have much choice in the matter," she admitted. "Jules doesn't like my scheme at all. He thinks I'm acting like a brazen hussy."

"Aren't you?" Tennant asked.

She resented that; and showed it in the tone of her voice. "I'm doing what I think necessary to save this ranch. If being brazen will help us win, I'll be brazen."

Presently she added, "I come by it honestly, Jeff. I'm Tate Usher's daughter."

Tennant stared at her. "You're what?" he demanded.

151

Leona smiled, as if enjoying his astonishment. She said, "I found it out the night Daddy Bell died. He was delirious, and he kept pleading with Tate Usher not to tell about me — not to let anyone know I was Usher's daughter. Afterward, when I took over the ranch records, I found several entries in a cash book marked loans to Tate Usher. They totaled eighteen thousand dollars, Jeff, which explains why TU got bigger while Bar Bell went downhill."

Tennant considered her startling revelation in shocked silence for several minutes. Then he said, "So that's why you told me no one else had so much reason for hating Tate Usher."

"Yes," Leona agreed, "and it's why I want to see TU shrunk back to a shirttail outfit. If being brazen will help do it, I'll be as brazen as one of Mayme Shay's girls."

Then, with a frankness that pleased Tennant, she added, "Dude's kisses aren't much of a price to pay, Jeff. In fact I rather like them."

Tennant chuckled. Here was a girl false enough to lure a man into becoming a spy, yet honest enough to admit she enjoyed his kisses. Considering this, Tennant understood that Dude Finn's brash courting was a new thing to Leona — that compared with Clark Morgan's disciplined correctness, Dude's bull boldness would have a certain appeal.

"So Finn is now a spy, along with being a ladies' man," Tennant reflected.

He was shaping up a cigarette when Leona

said, "Speaking of ladies' men reminds me that I've got more news for you, Jeff. Clark is courting Jane Medwick again."

The wheat-straw paper broke between Tennant's fingers. He peered at Leona while flakes of tobacco sifted to the floor, and asked, "How do you know that?"

"Doc came out to check on Jules yesterday. We got to talking about you, and I said it looked as if you'd left the country. Doc said he hoped you had, now that Clark was keeping company with Jane."

Tennant discarded the torn cigarette paper. He rubbed a thumb along his whisker-bristled chin and muttered, "So she thinks I shot Naviska in the back."

"Sure," Leona said. "So does everyone else."

"Do you?" Tennant asked.

Leona nodded. "Doc should be able to tell whether a man was shot in the back or not. But it makes no difference to me, one way or the other."

A mirthless smile twisted Tennant's lips. Leona thought he was questioning the fact Red was shot in the back — not who'd shot him. There was no doubt in her mind about his shooting Naviska, nor in anyone else's. He stood convicted without trial, even by Jane. That was the part he couldn't comprehend — that Jane would believe it. And that she would quit him without hearing his side of it. . . .

"I guess you had quite a case on Doc's

daughter," Leona said sympathetically. She crossed the kitchen and brought a bottle and a glass from the cupboard and suggested, "Drown your sorrow with a dose of Colonel's Monogram, Jeff."

Tennant took the generous portion at a gulp. *"Gracias,"* he said, and when she filled the glass again he gazed at the amber whiskey in silence for a brief interval, seeking a way to excuse Jane's lack of faith — wanting to save the precious image she had made for him. But he couldn't contrive it, nor hold back the resentment that came, wave on wave, to wash the image away.

He downed the second drink in moody silence. Leona refilled the glass, took a sip herself, and handed it to him with a self-mocking smile. "We're a couple of renegades," she said. "Let's be happy renegades."

Tennant grinned, and emptied the glass. Then he got up, saying, "Guess I'll head for the bunkhouse. Haven't had much sleep lately."

Leona walked to the door with him. When he opened it she placed a hand on his arm and said softly, "Jane wasn't your kind of woman, Jeff."

It occurred to Tennant now that Leona had lost Clark Morgan. He asked, "Was Morgan your kind of man?"

"I guess not," Leona said. Her hands came up to his shoulders and she whispered, "I guess you're my kind, Jeff."

And there was a smile on her pouty, half-parted lips when Tennant kissed her. . . .

154

17. No Quick Kisses

In saddle before daylight, Tennant reached the roundup camp in time to join Bar Bell's crew at breakfast. "We been expectin' you every night," Bravo Shafter announced cheerfully. "We knowed you'd give them galoots the dodge sooner or later."

Tennant grinned. "It took a little time," he admitted, and glancing at Joe Barlow, said, "So you're back in the cow business again."

"Yeah — and I'm stayin' in it, Jeff. That town life don't agree with me at all."

Joe looked more like his old self, Tennant thought; he looked proud, and so did young Billy who said now, "Town life is for wimminfolk."

Tennant wondered what Effie Barlow thought about this deal. The poor woman probably felt deserted, with Rose and her menfolk gone. The thought came to Tennant that he should send Joe and Billy back to her; that even though he hadn't hired them, he was morally responsible for their remaining here. But something he saw in Joe Barlow's eyes kept Tennant from interfering. Joe didn't look like a boozy old loafer now; he looked like a man. . . .

When the crew saddled up, Tennant asked, "How many more days to get the job done, Bravo?"

"Seven or eight," Shafter predicted.

Tennant peered across the scatteration of bedrolls to where the herd was being held by a slow-circling rider. It was full daylight now, the air raw with night's dampness and with the wind-toted chill of snow-mantled mountains.

"I figure five more days is all we can spare," Tennant announced. "Then we drive what we've got gathered."

Shafter shrugged. "You're the boss," he muttered.

Presently, as Tennant led his seven-man crew out for the day's circle, he said, "I may have to leave you boys on short notice, so I'd better tell you how this deal is to be handled. We finish the roundup Friday, and camp at Big Meadow. Friday night we drive the Bar Bell stuff toward TU —"

"Ain't you got your rope kinked?" Pete Lunsford asked.

Tennant shook his head. "That's our decoy herd," he explained. "While four men are driving it slow and easy the rest will be pushing Usher's steers up the Slot, through the Pass and over into the Crazy Canyons."

For a long moment, as the men considered this news, they rode in silence. Then Joe Barlow exclaimed, "Why, that's a peach of a scheme, Jeff — a jim-dandy!"

And Shafter said, "Usher wouldn't have a chance to bring back them steers in time to fill his Reservation contract."

"That's the way I figure it," Tennant agreed. "But we've got to make our drive through the Pass before snow gets drifted too deep."

"We'll do her," Billy Barlow declared. "Ain't nothin' can stop us, by grab!"

And so it seemed. For even though a drenching rain set in before noon, the day's gather was a good one. So good in fact that Tennant decided to move camp a day ahead of schedule. After supper he saddled a fresh horse, saying, "I've got to make a trip to town," and rode off at a mud-splashing lope. Leona, he believed, had told the truth about Jane. But he had to hear Jane's explanation for quitting without giving him a chance to clear himself. Even if she didn't believe what he was going to tell her, she owed him the chance to tell it.

Ben Petty's departure, he understood, had ruined all hope of proving that Usher had rigged the brand-plotting deal three years ago. There'd be no trial now — no chance to use those boot prints as evidence. By leaving Bunchgrass Basin Petty had as good as admitted himself guilty of Ed Peebles' killing. . . .

"And the spooky fool has spoiled the only chance I had to prove Usher framed me," Tennant muttered.

Afterward, as he neared Quadrille, Tennant recalled the romantic interlude he'd shared with Leona last night. Her passionate, eager embrace and her talk about his being her kind of man had both surprised and pleased him. But now he dismissed it for what he considered it to be: merely a brief and meaningless display of pent-up emotions. Leona had lived a lonely life. She liked attention, and wasn't particular who furnished it. If Dude Finn had happened by Bar Bell last night Leona would probably have welcomed him as warmly.

There was, Tennant reflected, plenty of reason for her being as she was. She had inherited Tate Usher's lack of principle and his selfishness. Even as Usher would use any trick to ruin Bar Bell, Leona would do the same to save it. Romance had been secondary with Tate, despite his hot-blooded ways. And it was the same with Leona. No man would ever come ahead of Bar Bell, Tennant reflected. The ranch was the thing Leona lived for; that and her hatred of the man who'd sired her.

It was still raining when Tennant tied his horse to the picket fence in front of Doc Medwick's house. The lamplit windows sent out a cheerful glow, and the tinkling notes of a piano reminded Tennant of the many evenings he'd spent in the parlor, listening to the soft, sweet music Jane loved to play. He wondered about Doc, and hoped the medico was with his cronies at the Palace.

A familiar eagerness prodded Tennant as he knocked on the front door. Anticipation, and a sudden warming sense of confidence, came to him while he waited. Jane had believed him that other time, in spite of the jury's decision; she would believe him now. All he had to do was to tell her the truth. It seemed as simple as that to Tennant now, and he was grinning cheerfully when Jane opened the door.

"Jeff!" she exclaimed.

Tennant took off his rain-soaked hat. He stepped inside and closed the door and asked, "Glad to see me, honey?"

"Why — yes," Jane said. "Of course."

Tennant gazed at her as if to fill his eyes with the pleasing picture she made for him. "The man," he said smilingly, "hadn't seen the girl for a long, long time."

Then, as he reached out to take her in his arms, Tennant saw Clark Morgan standing in the parlor doorway. . . .

In all his foot-loose years Jeff Tennant had never been jealous of any man. Now, for the first time, he was jealous — really, rampantly jealous. The swift burst of it was like a flame inside him.

Jane took his hat and said, "Take off your slicker, Jeff," and stood waiting for it.

But Tennant ignored her. He peered at Morgan and demanded, "What you doing here?"

"I was about to ask you the same question," Morgan said in his precise, orderly voice. "I thought you were dodging a posse back in the hills."

"Your mistake," Tennant muttered. He stepped away from the door, adding, "And your time to leave."

Morgan's glance shifted to Jane. He asked,

"Would you prefer that I leave?"

Tennant gave Jane no chance to answer that. Stepping close to Morgan he said brashly, "Let's decide it with our fists, Morgan."

"I don't choose to fight in this house," the merchant said with the patience of a thoroughly disciplined man — a patience that hugely aggravated Jeff Tennant.

"Maybe this will change your mind," Tennant said, and slapped Morgan's face.

"Why, Jeff — Jeff Tennant!" Jane objected indignantly.

But Clark Morgan possessed an established composure that nothing seemed to shake. He said again, "Not in this house." Then he took his hat and coat from the hall tree, said, "Good night, Jane," and went outside, closing the door gently behind him.

"Yellow," Tennant reflected. He turned to Jane, knowing that Morgan had outplayed him here and that the merchant's ironclad control had made his undisciplined display seem like cheap bravado. . . .

"Sorry I lost my temper," Tennant apologized, "but I'm not sorry Morgan left."

"Aren't you afraid the posse will find you here?" Jane asked coolly.

Tennant shook his head. He asked, "Is Lambert in town?"

"He was this morning," Jane said. She watched him go to the door and peer out, and leave it slightly ajar when he turned back to her.

He said, "I haven't much time, but I want you to know I didn't shoot Naviska — in the back or otherwise."

Jane met his unwavering gaze. She asked, "You wouldn't lie to me, would you, Jeff?"

A slow grin creased Tennant's whisker-bristled cheeks. He said, "I might, some time. But I never have. Naviska was shot by mistake. I think young Johnny Peebles mistook Red for Ben Petty. But, however it happened, I didn't do it."

Then, as hooftromp sounded in the street, Tennant turned quickly toward the doorway, his right hand hovering close to holster. Watching him now, Jane saw how much he'd changed in the past few days. He had a wary way with him; an alertness and a vigilance, as if this was a game he thoroughly understood. And thoroughly enjoyed. That was the part she couldn't comprehend — that he should take pleasure in so grisly a game.

A galloping horse splashed along the dark, rain-drenched road; when the muffled beat of its passage across the bridge came back, Tennant mused, "Someone in a hurry."

He stood in thoughtful silence for a moment, wondering who that rider might be. Then he said, "It's Morgan, going to tell Usher where I am."

The idea of Morgan riding into the hills on a night like this amused him. The merchant was in for a considerable wetting before he found the posse. Tennant smiled and asked, "You wouldn't marry an informer, would you, honey?"

Jane shrugged. She said, "I don't blame Clark for resenting your actions, Jeff. I resent them myself."

Then she asked, "Do you know that Joe Barlow and his boy are with the Bar Bell roundup crew?"

When he nodded, she asked, "Do you think that's right, after what you promised Effie?"

Tennant thought, *So Effie has been complaining. . . .*

He said, "I didn't hire them, Jane. But in my opinion Joe is better off riding roundup than guzzling booze at Stromberg's bar. And young Billy is doing what he's wanted to do for a long, long time."

"Suppose they get shot?" she asked. "Will that be better for them, also?"

Tennant frowned. Here it was, all over again. Jane disliked violence so thoroughly that she considered no price too great to pay for peace. "It's a chance they have to take," he explained, "unless they want to spend their lives tied to Effie's apron strings. A man can't always play it safe and secure, Jane. Even Morgan is risking his neck hightailing up that slippery road tonight."

But this didn't convince her at all. Tennant could tell by the way she looked at him, with her eyes so coolly calculating. He'd never seen that expression in her eyes. It wasn't like Jane to be calculating. Nor aloof. Even on the few occasions when she'd been angry at him she'd never been like this. . . .

He asked, "You believe me, about Naviska?"

"Yes, I believe you. But that doesn't change the rest of it, Jeff. It doesn't change the fact that you're willing to risk Joe Barlow's life and young Billy's to win yourself a bunch of cattle."

The unfairness of that roused swift resentment in Tennant. "I'm not fighting just for a bunch of cattle," he said impatiently. "There's more to it than that."

"Revenge?" Jane asked, and contrived to make the question an accusation as well.

Then her voice turned soft and warm and pleading as she asked, "Won't anything stop you, Jeff — before it's too late?"

Tennant was considering that, and taking hope from it, when he heard footsteps in the yard. Going to the door he glanced out and saw Doc Medwick. And understood that this visit was almost over. . . .

Whereupon he turned to Jane and took her by the shoulders and asked, "A quick kiss before I go?"

Jane shook her head. "No quick kisses, Jeff. That's all there'd ever be, the way you're going. That, and waiting to learn if you were dead or alive. It's no use, Jeff. I'm through waiting."

Doc Medwick came in. He said sternly, "Unless you need medical assistance go out and get on your horse."

Tennant ignored the old medico. He asked, "You sure about it, Jane?"

"Of course she's sure!" Medwick declared. "You've had your chance, Jeff — and you've chosen the gunsmoke game. Why should any sensible girl wait for a posse-dodging renegade to get caught — or killed!"

The measured ticking of the hallway clock sounded loud to Jeff Tennant. Tick, tock, while he looked at the only girl he'd ever wanted for a wife. Tick, tock, while he waited for his answer, and read it in the appraising coolness of her eyes. Tick, tock. . . .

"Get out," Doc ordered.

There was no anger in his voice. Just impatience, and a little disgust. The tone of voice a man might use on a grubline rider who'd overstayed his welcome. . . .

A mirthless grin twisted Tennant's lips. This was the way you lost a beautiful woman. With a clock ticking and an old man telling you to get out. No chance to fight for her with your fists, or with a gun. No opportunity to take her in your arms and kiss her objections away.

Tennant took his hat from Jane and said gruffly, "I could wish you luck with Morgan, but I'd be lying. I'd be lying like hell."

Then he strode outside, slamming the door behind him.

18. Belly Down

Bravo Shafter couldn't understand it. Each day the gather increased and the roundup was ahead of schedule, yet Jeff Tennant's morose mood continued. He seldom spoke, except to give an order; even when Leona visited camp on the third day and talked to Jeff he didn't seem to say much.

Billy Barlow noticed it, for he asked his father, "You reckon Jeff has a bellyache, or somethin'?"

But if Tennant was sick he didn't reveal it in his actions. First to saddle up in the morning he was last to fill his plate at Shakespear Smith's supper fire, and he rode the slick, slippery hills with a reckless speed that made Old Pete Lunsford remark, "A ridge-runnin' rannihan. Puts me in mind of my younger days in Texas."

On Thursday afternoon Tennant took a tally of the herd. And because this was the first time the overcast had lifted, he also took a long look at the Divide's white mantle. There was snow down to the Slot. Even if it wasn't deep it would make for treacherous footing and slow progress up the steep trail.

This was at Big Meadow. The last circles were being made, with small bunches of cattle drifting in from the roundabout hills as riders choused them through brush and pine timber. . . .

"Hi-ya, cattle! Hi-ya, hi-ya!"

Weary men riding weary horses, cursing the

bunch-quitter steers; cursing the mud that spattered their beard-shagged faces.

"Git along, cattle — git along!"

The cutting was started while riders were still
out on circle. Slow, tedious, temper-ragging
work that churned the meadow bottom into a
hock-deep sludge of mud and manure where
pivoting ponies went down and swearing men
kicked mud-caked boots free of stirrups. Within
an hour one horse was so badly gored it had to be
shot, and soon after that young Billy Barlow
limped up to the wagon with a horn-slashed leg
for Shakespear Smith to bandage. But the work
went on, TU steers to the west side of the
meadow, Bar Bell stuff to the east; hour after
hour of it, while Jack Ramsay brought in eleven
head and Bravo Shafter showed up just before
dark with six more.

"Had nine to start with," Bravo admitted wearily, "but three of 'em turned back on me."

Then he added, "Saw a rider headin' toward
Bar Bell. Looked like Dude Finn."

Tennant thought about that for a moment. If
Shafter had seen Finn it must mean the posse
had returned, and Dude might be making a
report of Usher's plans to Leona. . . .

He said, "Take over till I get back, Bravo. Eat
supper soon as the cut is finished, and start the
two herds moving. You, the Barlows and Fred
Eggleston handle the TU steers. I'll catch up
with the other boys, and we'll try to join you
some time before daylight. But no matter what

166

happens, push those steers through the Pass."

Then, not waiting for Shafter's acceptance of this, Tennant turned his horse toward Bar Bell. Bravo, he thought, might question his being sent with the steers instead of the Bar Bell herd, which was where the fighting would be — if there was a fight. But Tennant wanted him to ramrod the drive up the Slot Trail. That was the important part of this deal; the part that meant survival or ruin for Bar Bell — and for himself.

It was dark when Tennant topped the first ridge west of the roundup camp. Cow smell came off the meadow, strongly pungent in the damp air. Smith's supper fire made a meager shine against the dark and there was no cheer in the sight of it; no sense of warmth or fellowship for Jeff Tennant. It occurred to him now that there'd been none of that since the night Jane had refused to wait for him.

He had known then that he'd lost her. But there was a flimsy strand of hope in him until Leona visited camp and reported that a wedding day had been set. "Jane is wearing Clark's diamond," she'd told him. "They're to be married on the fifteenth and Doc is bragging that it'll be the biggest wedding ever put on in Bunchgrass Basin."

And the best, to Doc's way of thinking, Tennant thought morosely. There'd never been a time when the old medico had wanted him for a son-in-law. Doc was a town man and wanted his daughter to marry a man who'd live in town. A

167

peaceable, prominent citizen who could give Jane the comforts and security she was accustomed to having.

"That's what Jane wants also," Tennant muttered.

A three-quarter moon was shining through wind-raveled clouds when he rode into the Bar Bell yard. There was a saddled horse tied to the back stoop; he passed close enough to see its TU brand, and thought, *Bravo was right!*

Leona, he guessed, would be entertaining Dude in the kitchen while Jules Huffmeyer remained in the parlor, for there were lamps going in both rooms. He wondered about Finn's reaction to this meeting, and regretted the necessity of revealing his connection with Bar Bell. But if the TU rider had news of Usher's immediate plans it might make considerable difference in the outcome of tonight's high-stake game. . . .

Tennant tied his horse to the corral fence and was walking across the moonlit yard when he heard Leona cry, "No, Dude — no!"

The sheer surprise of it held him motionless for a moment, and in this brief interval Leona screamed.

Tennant rushed to the kitchen door. He flung it open, saw Leona struggling with Finn — and glimpsed Jules Huffmeyer sprawled near the parlor doorway with blood on his forehead.

Leona's hair was down and her dress was torn from shoulders that gleamed bare in the lamplight. She cried, "Jeff!" and that single word freed her at once from Dude Finn's embrace.

Finn drew as he whirled, and fired one frantic, half-aimed shot before Tennant's gun exploded. Dude's gun slipped from his fingers and both hands clutched spasmodically at his chest. He took three queerly graceful steps backward. Then he bent at the middle, as if taking a bow, and fell so abruptly that his face thudded against the floor.

Afterward, while Leona doctored Huffmeyer whom Finn had pistol-whipped, Tennant toted Dude's body outside and coaxed the TU bronc to stand while he tied the limp shape to saddle, belly down. Handling the body made Tennant sick. He gagged, and cursed himself for this squeamishness. Hell, he'd shot two men during the Lincoln County War, hadn't he? It wasn't as if this was his first gun fight. But those other shootings had been during an impersonal battle between strangers. This seemed worse, somehow. Even though he had fired in self-defense it seemed worse. . . .

Tennant turned the horse loose and hazed it from the yard. The thought came to him that Usher would accuse him of this killing as a matter of course, and that Jane would soon hear the news. If there'd been any last doubt in her mind about marrying Morgan, this would clinch it, he supposed. She might even wonder if he'd lied to her about Red Naviska.

When Tennant returned to the stoop Leona

stood there waiting for him. She wore a coat cape-fashion around her shoulders but it didn't conceal the torn bodice of her dress nor the white swell of partially exposed breasts. . . .

"You killed him to save me, didn't you, Jeff," she said softly.

"No," Tennant muttered, resenting the satisfied smile on her face now. "I killed him to save myself."

It seemed odd that a girl should smile at a time like this; that she should seem pleased and wholly self-contained so soon after seeing a man killed. A man whose kisses she'd enjoyed.

Tennant asked, "Did Finn know when Usher plans to jump the herd?"

"Yes, but Dude wanted to — to be paid, before he told me."

Tennant laughed cynically. "So all your scheming got you was a torn dress," he taunted.

Leona wasn't smiling now. She was peering at him with wide, startled eyes. "But I did it for both of us, Jeff," she insisted.

"Us?"

Leona reached out and grasped his arms. "Of course," she said, and smiled again. "You're going to share Bar Bell with me, aren't you?"

Until this moment it hadn't occurred to Jeff Tennant that she would marry him. Even though she had called him her kind of man he'd considered their brief intimacy an emotional interlude sparked by mutual disappointment, and by more whisky than he was used to drinking.

Certainly there had been no mention of love, no matrimonial intent. Even now, with the knowledge that she was offering him a full partnership, he thought, *She's lost Morgan and wants me as second best.*

Her nails tightened so that her nails bit into his arms. She asked invitingly, "Aren't you, Jeff?"

And her eyes, so warmly glowing, told him that she was offering more than half of Bar Bell. . . .

Tennant thought about this, taking time to place an accurate reckoning on his future and knowing how forlorn a place Roman Four would be without Jane to share it. Here was a woman wanting a mate; wanting a partner, too. If they won the fight against Usher, Bar Bell would be bigger than ever — a vast cattle kingdom. And he had nothing to lose by such an alliance, except what tattered remnants of pride Jane had left him.

Yet, for a reason he couldn't understand, Tennant said finally, "Our bargain was one hundred heifers and five bulls. I see no need for changing it."

Leona's hands dropped instantly. She stepped back and stared at him, demanding, "You mean — you don't want me?"

Tennant shrugged. He said, "There's only one girl I ever really wanted. Nothing will change that."

"Not even her marriage to Clark Morgan?" Leona asked, incredulous.

"Nothing will change my wanting her," Tennant said and walked to his horse.

Leona remained on the stoop as he rode past, and because she was thoroughly angry her lamplit face held a graphic, passionate beauty. She was the living image of a desirable woman now. She roused a rash urge in Jeff Tennant, an itching impulse to turn back and take her in his arms.

But he didn't.

19. An Unexpected Warning

Goldie Rimbaugh rode into Menafee Camp shortly after eight o'clock. He said to Cleek, "They cut the herd this afternoon and they're driving a bunch this way."

"How far back?" Cleek asked, picking at his gold teeth with a match stick.

"Five-six miles. It was dark when they lined out right after supper. But I seen Jeff Tennant workin' the cuts this afternoon."

"So that's where he's been the past few days," Tate Usher muttered. "While we was freezin' up there in the snow Tennant was down here just like Clark Morgan told us."

Lee Pardee said, "He's a smart one, that Tennant. I remember a foxy trick he turned whilst ridin' in that Lincoln County fracas. He was —"

"To hell with that," Cleek interrupted crankily. "I'm sick of hearin' how goddam smart that jigger is."

He turned to Rimbaugh and asked, "Where's Dude?"

"Can't figger it out," Rimbaugh said. "Dude told me to wait while he made a circle south of Big Meadow. He never come back."

"You hear any shots?" Cleek asked.

Rimbaugh shook his head. "When Dude didn't show back I thought mebbe he went on into town for a drink. Dude likes his likker."

"Also his wimmin," Lee Pardee offered with a chuckle. "If you opened up Dude's head all you'd find would be a naked woman spraddled out on a blanket."

Kid Peebles stood in the doorway with an oil-soaked rag and a revolver in his hands. "Dude," he suggested, "might be at Mayme Shay's place right now, havin' hisself a time."

"I'll fire that proddy bum, traipsin' off when we need him," Usher threatened.

Then, as a horse sloshed through mud puddles near by, Cleek said sharply, "Look what's coming!"

Rimbaugh exclaimed, "That's Dude's horse!"

"And Dude's body on it," Cleek predicted.

The pony came on, stepping high through the yard's deep mud.

"God A'mighty!" Kid Peebles blurted, staring at the limp head and mud-spattered hands that dangled loosely.

The pony stopped at the corral gate. It gave a low nicker, as if asking to be relieved of its gruesome burden. Idaho Cleek walked over and grasped Dude's hair and tilted the face for a brief look.

"Is it Dude?" Usher called.

"Who the hell'd you think it was — General Grant?" Cleek snapped. Then he peered at the doorway group and called impatiently, "Come on, come on. Cut the corpse loose and tote it into the shack."

Rimbaugh and Pardee went about the chore

with reluctance. Goldie took out his knife and said regretfully, "Old Dude won't be makin' no more town trips to have his ashes hauled."

When Cleek came up, Usher complained, "We play it legal much longer and we'll need a whole new crew."

"Play it any other way and you won't need a crew," Cleek retorted. "We've got Lambert with us, haven't we? How long would you've lasted in this country if the sheriff had been against you?"

Usher sighed. "I know, but we ain't gittin' what we're after, Idaho. We ain't no nearer Bar Bell headquarters than we was a year ago."

"Oh, yes we are," Cleek corrected. "We've got Petty's place, haven't we? And Jeff Tennant is as good as run off his, which means we control the Tailholt Hills."

"But we got to git Tennant first, by God!" Usher exclaimed. "If he should throw in with Bar Bell there's no telling what might happen."

Cleek smiled. He rolled a cigarette and watched Finn's body being carried into the cabin.

Kid Peebles watched also. He had never liked Dude, but the way Dude's head wobbled with the mouth wide open made Johnny feel bad. "I wonder who'll be next," he said sickishly.

Usher asked, "What'll we do about that drive, Idaho?"

"Bust it," Cleek said. "Bust it good and proper."

"How about Lambert? What'll he think about that?"

"You heard Goldie say Tennant is working with the Bar Bell crew, didn't you?" Cleek asked impatiently. "That makes Bar Bell an outlaw crew."

Usher peered thoughtfully at his foreman. "Sure," he agreed. "Sure it does."

"And we're all sworn in as deputies, to take Tennant dead or alive," Cleek said, as if explaining an intricate problem to a child.

Usher smacked his chap-clad leg. "Then we can bust 'em legal!" he exclaimed.

Cleek smiled thinly and glanced at the cloud-mottled sky. "If it don't storm for a couple hours we'll have good targets, Tate. Lots of good targets."

When they walked to the corral to saddle up, Usher said worriedly, "We'll be outnumbered a trifle, Idaho."

"Not after the first couple minutes, we won't be," Cleek promised. "We're going to make those first shots count, and I don't want anybody firing till I give the word."

Afterward, as they rode from the yard, Cleek looked at the sky again and said, "I hope the moonlight lasts one more hour."

Both herds had left Big Meadow when Tennant rode up to the chuck wagon where Shakespear Smith crouched close to a glowing bed of embers.

"The north herd started out right after supper," Smith reported grouchily. "Shafter got moving about an hour ago. He said I'm supposed to be at Bent Elbow and have breakfast ready at sunup. Is that official?"

Tennant nodded. "They'll want a pack horse loaded with provision for the trip up to the Pass. After that you can roll for home."

The old cook slumped closer to the fire, holding his bearded face in both hands. "It's ghastly," he complained. "Fifteen years on the stage entertaining multitudes of ardent admirers — twenty years of culinary triumph cooking in cow camps, and my reward is an all-night drive in shivering solitude."

Smith lifted tragic eyes to consider shifting cloudbanks, and added, "A big storm brewing, which means I'll probably be wheeling through a blizzard by the time I reach Bent Elbow."

Tennant rode on, feeling a kindred moroseness and not wanting to share it. There was a storm brewing, all right. Two storms, in fact. For he felt sure that Usher had sent men to scout the roundup's progress and they would've witnessed the start of the north drive. Which meant that one of the storms would break before midnight.

The moon shone intermittently, its periods of illumination less frequent as Tennant splashed along the road which had been churned into a quagmire by the herd's recent passage. A stronger wind came out of the north, raw and damp with a smell of snow in it. Pine timber made a windbreak here, and a sort of barrier on both sides of the road. Lunsford, Ramsay and Taylor should have had little trouble driving cattle through here, Tennant thought. And they had been told to take it easy.

When he overtook Pete Lunsford dawdling behind slow-plodding drags, the old man asked, "Find out anything at the ranch?"

Tennant shook his head and rode on without speaking, but he thought, *I found out how it feels to kill at close range.* He had learned also how unpredictable his reactions could be. Recalling the contrasting emotions Leona had aroused in him, Tennant felt a nagging sense of bewilderment. A man could never be sure of himself around a woman. He could despise her with half his mind and want her with the other half. . . .

He rode alongside Jack Ramsay and asked, "How they acting?"

"Just like they'd been drove all their life," Ramsay bragged. Then he asked, "How far you reckon we'll get before TU tackles us?"

"Quién sabe?" Tennant said and made the shrugging gesture which is part of this Spanish declaration of doubt. "We're on Usher's range now. He might let us get beyond Menafee Camp, or he might jump us in the next ten minutes."

It occurred to him that there were half a dozen likely places for ambush. Making a mental tally of the trail's crooked course through the hills he thought about those places, and wondered which of them Usher would choose. The cut-bank pass on the ridge near Menafee Camp, perhaps; or the timber-fringed gully beyond it. . . .

Then he remembered Nugget Wash. That, too, would be a natural trap. And it wasn't far off. Calculating the time it would take the herd to reach it, Tennant guessed that they'd be there in another fifteen or twenty minutes.

He said, "Don't forget how the plan goes, Jack. Soon as the shooting starts we drop back and make a slow fight. The longer it lasts the better. Only thing we're trying to win is time."

He rode ahead then, intending to guard against cattle turning down Nugget Wash instead of crossing it.

"Keep your eyes peeled," Ramsay advised. "I got a hunch that wash might be the place."

The moon was half hidden by clouds now, so that the herd was little more than a blur of moving shadows. Tennant passed the leaders and glimpsed Tex Taylor moving up through the trees across the trail. Tex, he supposed, was wondering about Nugget Wash also. It was directly ahead, not more than a hundred yards away. The timber petered out and was replaced by brush and boulders. Even in this poor light the sandy bottom made a wide chalky strip between the dark banks above it.

Tennant scanned those brush-fringed banks, the sense of impending attack so strong now that he expected to see movement up there. But he detected no sign of ambush as he rode into the wash and turned his horse down it far enough to allow the herd to cross without interference.

The leaders came on, sniffed at the wet sand and plodded methodically across it. When three cows turned up the wash Taylor yelled "Hi-ya — hi-ya!" and quickly sent them back into the herd.

"Go on cattle — go on," Tennant chanted again and again, slapping his saddle with a rope end.

Most of the herd was across and moving up the steep trail beyond. Lunsford urged the last stragglers into the wash, and Tennant thought, *This isn't the place.*

Tension ran out of him. It would take another hour to reach the cut-bank pass; perhaps longer. And like he'd told his companions, time was all they had to win. He took his Durham sack from his pocket and began shaping a cigarette with cold-numbed fingers. Jack Ramsay was helping old Pete with the drags, cursing the cattle in a singsong voice.

Tennant lit the cigarette and at this exact instant heard Idaho Cleek call sharply from the high bank, "Grab your gun, Tennant!"

That challenge astonished Tennant. He had anticipated gunfire without warning — had expected that the shrill whine of a bullet would signal attack. But even so, with surprise hurtling through him, Tennant had his horse in motion when guns began blasting above him.

As the first bullet whanged past his face he thought, *Cleek had me lined in his sights,* and wondered why TU's foreman had taken the trouble to challenge him.

Tennant drew his gun and was firing at the bright beacons of muzzle flare above him when a bullet burned into his left thigh. He pressed the wound instinctively with his rein hand and cursed the splinters of pain that spiraled up his leg. Then a slug gouged a hank of hide from his horse's flank. The animal squealed, bogged its head and crossed the wash in a wild tantrum of bucking.

They were into timber when Tennant got the horse under control. There was a lull in the firing now, and Tennant heard Pete Lunsford yell, "Back here, Tex — back here!"

Another burst of shooting, then Tex Taylor's shrill, high-pitched scream came from up the wash.

Tennant thought, *He's gut-shot*, and winced as Taylor screamed again.

20. A Shift in the Wind

The moonlight faded out completely. Tennant heard cattle stampede back across the wash as he eased his horse through the timber. He wondered about Tex. There'd been no more yelling, and no more shooting. Wind-blown rain spattered against his face; when he turned into the road his horse lunged sideways abruptly, narrowly missing collision with a cow brute that went splashing past.

Presently Tennant called, "Where are you, Pete?"

"Over here," Lunsford said.

Tennant couldn't see him, but the tone of the old man's voice made him suspicious at once; so he asked, "You hurt?"

"Some," Lunsford admitted. "Right arm is no goddam good."

Tennant rode up beside Lunsford who made a vague, saddle-slumped shape in the rain-swept darkness. "I'll fix you a tourniquet," he said and cut a saddle string for that purpose.

"Tex got it," the old man muttered. "He stayed out there in the wash instead of droppin' back like he was supposed to."

"Maybe he's just wounded," Tennant said. "I'll go take a look soon as I fix your arm."

When he tied the tourniquet, Pete said, "Usher played it smart, lettin' us all git into the wash before they started shootin'."

"Yeah," Tennant agreed, "but I can't figure out why Cleek yelled at me like he did."

"Mebbe he can't kill a man cold turkey," Lunsford suggested.

The same explanation had occurred to Tennant but he had discarded it. A man of Cleek's caliber wouldn't adhere to a code of fair play after setting an ambush trap. . . .

The tromp of a near-by horse brought Tennant instantly alert. He had his gun drawn when Jack Ramsay rode up and announced, "Tex is dead."

"You sure?" Tennant asked.

"Yeah. Tex got shot off'n his horse. I seen him and was goin' out to help, but a bunch of them big steers tromped Tex all to hell."

Ramsay gagged. He said whimperingly, "Never saw such a God-awful sight."

Tennant shivered, and noticed that the rain had turned to snow.

"What do we do now?" Lunsford asked.

Tennant didn't answer for a moment. He forced his thoughts away from Tex Taylor. He listened to the wind prowl through the timber, and wondered if Usher's crew had left their perch. He squinted his eyes against the increasing flurry of snow flakes, half expecting to see riders loom against the yonder darkness.

Finally he said, "Ride to the ranch with Pete, then go get Doc Medwick to fix his arm."

"How about you?" Lunsford asked.

"I'll watch here for a spell," Tennant said. "If TU doesn't show up, I'll go give the boys a hand with the steers."

"We goin' to leave Tex's body there all night?" Ramsay asked.

"Nothing else we can do," Tennant muttered.

When they rode off he took out his knife, intending to cut a saddle string for a tourniquet, but the knife slipped from his cold-clumsy fingers. He cursed and dismounted into puddled mud that was fetlock deep. He tried to light a match but wind and snow frustrated three attempts, whereupon he blindly fingered the muck without success. Climbing back into saddle he wondered if the wound was still bleeding, and guessed it was. But the pain had dulled into an ache that sheathed his leg from knee to hip.

A hard gust of wind set up a high wail in the pines. It reminded him of Tex Taylor's scream. He waited and listened, sure that Usher's bunch had left their perch. If they didn't show soon he'd know they had called it a night. In which case the decoy herd had served its purpose, for those TU steers should be well up the Slot Trail by midmorning.

Tennant shrugged deeper into his mackinaw collar and waited out another ten minutes while his horse kept turning its tail to the wind. Then, as he was on the point of leaving, Tennant caught the wind-borne rumor of near-by voices.

Not waiting for a target, Tennant fired; he gigged his horse across the road and back, firing at split-second intervals to give the impression that two or three riders were in action. When his gun was empty he eased into the timber and re-loaded while TU riders opened up with a round of random firing.

Presently, as the shooting ceased, Tennant fired a single shot and trotted his horse deeper into the pines, smiling a little at the outburst of firing behind him. If Usher's bunch kept this up there'd be little chance of them bothering the steer herd tonight. And tomorrow would be too late.

For a time, as he rode a slow circle through the snow-pelted darkness, Tennant considered the changes this night's work might bring to Bunchgrass Basin. Usher would be ruined financially by failure to fill his Indian Agency contract. A bankrupt outfit couldn't pay gun wages, which meant the end of his hard-case crew.

Just a matter of time, Tennant thought, and considering all this, briefly forgot the throbbing ache in his wounded leg. With TU shrunk to a one-man outfit Bar Bell would be the big spread, and Roman Four, the second-biggest. There'd be a chance for men like Joe Barlow to run cattle in the Tailholt Hills again. Ben Petty might come back to stand trial, in which case Tate Usher could be exposed as the scoundrel who'd framed a homesteader into Yuma Prison.

But because Jane was marrying Clark Morgan on the fifteenth, Tennant savored the satisfaction of tonight's success with no sense of jubilation. Roman Four, without Jane to share it, would be a sorry place regardless of how big an outfit it became. . . .

Tennant halted his horse behind a windfall and waited for sound of pursuit. Usher, he guessed, wasn't satisfied with killing one Bar Bell rider; TU's boss wanted more blood. It occurred to Tennant now that he was the one Usher really wanted.

"That's why he's making his crew buck this storm," Tennant mused and took satisfaction in that knowledge.

Afterward, hearing no sound of riders, he quartered toward Big Meadow. The wind whined shrilly through treetops; when he crossed a clearing snowflakes pelted the right side of his face.

It's getting worse, he thought, and wondered how Bravo Shafter was making out with the steer herd. The wind had been coming out of the north, but now it seemed to be shifting. He skirted Big Meadow and headed westward, and now the wind was full in his face. Within an hour his horse was lunging through frequent drifts and Tennant realized that Shakespear Smith might not be able to reach Bent Elbow with the wagon. That would mean there'd be no hot coffee for cold, saddle-beat riders tomorrow morning; no Dutch-oven breakfast to renew their ebbing vitality. But it wouldn't be the first time that men had been forced to drive cattle on empty stomachs.

When Tennant came to the abandoned chuck wagon stalled in a hub-deep drift he wasn't surprised. But later he met three snow-draped steers drifting eastward, and thought urgently, *Bravo is having trouble.* A nagging sense of apprehension caused him to urge his horse to a faster gait. The wind came in thrusting gusts that blinded him for minutes at a time and his tired horse invariably swerved southward during these wild squalls of snow-shrouded blankness.

Tennant used the wind-driven snow as a compass to keep him on course. When it pelted his right cheek he understood that his horse had drifted to a southwesterly direction, and forced the animal to the right until the snow came squarely against his face.

He thought, *Bravo is needing help right now,* and spurred his horse into a floundering gallop. Then, during a brief lull in the wind, he saw more steers — a whole bunch of ghostly gray shapes plodding methodically through the snow's slanting curtain.

Tennant knew then that he had lost. And knew why. A shift in the wind had defeated him. The steers had balked at facing the storm and Shafter had failed to hold them, once they turned tail to it. That failure meant that the roundup — all those mud-spattered days of tedious toil — had been futile. It meant that Tex Taylor's death and Pete Lunsford's bullet-broken arm and the burning core of pain in his own leg stood for nothing. Worse than nothing, for it had cost him the only girl he'd ever really wanted.

Tennant cursed, and rode on, meeting more steers. The herd, he supposed, had fanned out across a wide area. But they'd all head east, and Bar Bell's riders would go south. Yet even so, he had to be sure — had to know positively that the crew had quit.

At first daylight, with the wind-swept whiteness of Bent Elbow Canyon below him, Jeff Tennant knew.

There wasn't a steer, nor a rider in sight. . . .

It was easier, riding with the wind. Even though his horse was too leg-weary for anything faster than a plodding walk, the trip back seemed faster to Tennant. Perhaps it was because there was no hurry now, no need beyond the need for sleep. And a bandage for his leg. And a long drink of whiskey.

I'll get drunk, he thought morosely, *stinking drunk,* and was eager to reach Quadrille. But when he came to Ben Petty's place he put his horse in the lean-to shed and built a fire in the cabin. The stove's quick heat melted snow that had sifted in beneath the door, and it made Tennant so drowsy that he could scarcely keep awake long enough to wash and bandage his leg. The puckered wound was raw and inflamed; the flesh around it discolored.

"Needs Doc Medwick's attention," Tennant muttered.

By the looks of his pants leg the wound had bled a pint or more. That, he supposed, was the reason he felt so damn washed out. And so sleepy.

He wondered if Medwick was at Bar Bell, or had returned to town. Doc might have stayed at the ranch all night, because of the storm. As coroner he'd have to take a look at what was left of Tex Taylor, and if any of Usher's crew had been hit in last night's shooting the old medico might be at TU. . . .

Tennant eased back on the bunk to think about this, and was asleep almost instantly.

It had been a long night for Leona Bell. A tedious night. Fearful that Jules' skull might be fractured she had ridden to town for Doc Medwick. One hour after their return to Bar Bell Pete Lunsford had ridden in with a bullet-smashed arm and the news of Tex Taylor's death. Then Bravo Shafter had brought his frost-bitten crew home to tell her how completely the storm had ruined the steer drive.

"We couldn't hold 'em," he muttered dully. "We just couldn't hold 'em."

The crew had ridden out at daylight in search of Shakespear Smith, and Doc Medwick had gone to bed. But there was no sleeping for Leona — no escape from the constant, sickening realization that her fight against Tate Usher had failed.

"Damn him!" she sobbed, and finished off a cup of black coffee spiked with Colonel's Monogram — her third since breakfast.

A howling wind blew sleety snow against the kitchen's west window. The wind, she thought bitterly, would drive all those TU steers back to Tonto Flats. There'd be no chance of saving her winter graze now. No chance of saving anything.

Methodically, with the need for motion prodding her, Leona cleared the table of dirty dishes. Where, she wondered, was Jeff Tennant? It occurred to her that he might have been killed, but that possibility scarcely registered against the thrusting fear that she would lose Bar Bell — that she couldn't prevent the ruin Clark Morgan had predicted.

She was washing dishes at the sink when she saw Idaho Cleek ride across the snow-swept yard. He peered at the bunkhouse, keeping a wary watch on its door as he rode around toward the kitchen stoop.

Leona dried her hands on a dish towel. This, she knew instinctively, was an emergency call for Doc Medwick, but she thought with a rising excitement, *He might be like Dude Finn,* and hastily arranged her hair. When the knock came at the door she called, "Come in," and leaned indolently against the sink, shoulders back and hands on hips.

Cleek stepped inside, not removing his hat, and said, "Johnny Peebles is bad hurt. Is Doc Medwick here?"

Leona nodded. "Doc was up most of the night. He's sleeping."

"Somebody get hurt?" Cleek inquired slyly.

And when Leona nodded again, he asked, "Tennant?"

"No, Jeff hasn't been seen since you ambushed him at Nugget Wash."

"Too bad," Cleek said, without sarcasm. He walked over to the stove and stood there as Dude Finn had done that first night, holding his palms to the heat. But there was none of Dude's brash eagerness in this man's pale blue eyes, and Leona thought, *He's cold, inside and out.*

"That trick with the decoy herd fooled us," Cleek said. "We didn't find out about it until after daylight."

All the futile, frustrating anger of the past hours rose in Leona now. It flamed in her cheeks and put a harshness in her voice when she exclaimed, "It took a damned blizzard to beat me!"

Cleek eyed her with an increased interest. He said, "So you're smart enough to know you're licked. I wondered about that."

"No," Leona objected. "If Jeff Tennant is alive there's still a chance of stopping Tate Usher."

"How?" Cleek asked.

"With a bullet."

Cleek shrugged. "Could be," he admitted, and smiled thinly before asking, "Will you go tell Doc he's needed at TU?"

Leona was halfway across the kitchen when she stopped and faced Cleek and asked abruptly, "Would you be interested in owning half of Bar Bell?"

Cleek blinked in frank astonishment. Then he glanced at the whiskey bottle and said with sly derision, "There never was a woman could honey-fuss me for a fool, drunk or sober. Go get Doc Medwick."

21. Not Proudly

Hobo Bill Wimple sat at the oilcloth-covered table in Mayme Shay's kitchen and studied the wrinkled, dirt-smudged map before him — a cryptic *derrotero* purporting to be a chart to the famous Conquistador Cache. Crude drawings of mountains, trees, metates, wagon wheels and crosses were among the myriad symbols, many of which now bore penciled circles. . . .

"Look, Mayme," Wimple said, pointing proudly to the circles. "Look what I've accomplished in ten years' time — explored over half the places where the treasure chest could be buried. You know what that means?"

Mayme Shay smiled and shook her head and asked, "What, Bill?"

"Why, it means I'll find that hidden treasure in six or seven more years at the outside. Then I'm goin' to build you the biggest opry house betwixt Kansas City and San Francisco, so's it'll hold the crowds of people that'll flock to see the prettiest gal who ever danced on a stage!"

Mayme patted his shoulder, and said, "I'm some older than I was when the Bazaar closed, Bill. Fifteen years older."

"And prettier," Hobo Bill insisted. He pulled her onto his lap and kissed her and exclaimed, "By grab, Mayme, you git prettier every year. I never saw the beat of it."

When he kissed her again, Mayme closed her eyes and hugged him tight. "You're sweet as sugar," she said softly. "You make me feel like a scatterheels girl getting her first kiss in the moonlight."

They remained like that for a little time, while the teakettle sang merrily on the stove and a gusty wind rattled the kitchen windows. Then a bell, attached to the front door by a rope and pulley arrangement, jangled briefly.

"Business," Mayme said. She went out to the hallway and called, "Company, girls," as she passed the stairs.

Then she saw Jeff Tennant limp across the parlor and exclaimed, "Good God, kid — you been shot!"

A whimsical smile creased Tennant's haggard, whisker-stubbled cheeks as Mayme and Hobo Bill helped him upstairs. "There's a deputy on Doc Medwick's veranda," he explained, "and Lambert is watching McGonigle's Livery, so I came here."

Three kimono-clad girls stood in the upstairs hallway watching this, their painted faces tense with interest. . . .

When Tennant was in Mayme's room and sitting on the edge of her big bed, she looked at his blood-stained pants leg and asked, "How bad is it, Jeff?"

"Needs cauterizing, I guess."

Then a sheepish grin eased his fever-flaked lips and he said, "I could sure use a drink of whiskey, if you've got a bottle hid away."

"I'll go git it," Hobo Bill declared. "Colonel's Monogram — guaranteed to cure snake bite, frostbite and broken bones."

Mayme said, "I'll have one of the girls heat some water, while I go get Doc Medwick."

"How about that deputy?" Tennant asked. "I wouldn't want Usher's crew coming in here after me. Might mess up your place."

Mayme smiled and patted his shoulder. "Don't you worry about it, kid. I'll make out like one of my girls has been took with a bad case of appendicitis."

She went out into the hall and announced, "He's a personal friend of mine, kids — and I don't want anyone to know he's here. One of you put on a big pan of water to heat, and make him some coffee, while I go get Doc Medwick."

Clark Morgan ate a leisurely supper in the Palace dining room and presently, as he paid his bill at the lobby desk, he asked Effie Barlow, "Where's your menfolks? I heard they came home this afternoon."

"Billy is in bed with a hurt leg and a cold that's likely to turn into grippe," Mrs. Barlow reported. "Joe headed straight for Stromberg's bar — said he hadn't had a drink since he left."

"They're lucky to be alive, from what I hear," Morgan said. "Tex Taylor and Dude Finn were killed outright and they say Johnny Peebles is dying."

Effie sighed. "It's a terrible thing, all the trouble one man can cause. And there'll be no peace until he's caught — or killed."

Morgan nodded agreement and went out to the street. When he passed the livery he saw Sheriff Lambert standing in the doorway, talking to Tay McGonigle.

"Any news of Tennant?" Morgan called.

"They tracked him from Petty's shack, until the snow petered out," Lambert said. "He was headed this way."

Morgan went on to Doc Medwick's house and nodded a wordless greeting to Goldie Rimbaugh who sat well back in the veranda shadows smoking a cigarette.

"Miss Medwick ain't home," Rimbaugh reported. "Mayme Shay came after Doc for one of her girls that's awful sick. Doc not bein' home, Miss Medwick went instead."

"So," Morgan mused, and turned back down the steps.

Afterwards, as he neared McGonigle's Livery, he stopped abruptly and said, "I wonder," and saw that Tay was alone now.

Crossing the street to the stable, Morgan asked, "Where's Sam?"

"Went over to the hotel for a cup of coffee," the liveryman said, and when Morgan turned away, asked, "Something up?"

"I'm not sure," Morgan said, precise as always. "But I have a suspicion that Jeff Tennant may be hiding at Mayme Shay's place."

196

Tay McGonigle watched Morgan walk hurriedly toward the hotel. "A plague on ye," he whispered, and crossed Main Street with disciplined casualness. But once into Sashay Alley the little Irishman ran as fast as the sucking mud would allow. He was so out of breath that he could scarcely speak when he barged into Mayme Shay's parlor and found Hobo Bill coming from the kitchen with a pitcher of hot water.

"Is Jeff here?" Tay demanded wheezingly.

Hobo Bill eyed him with obvious surprise. "Jeff who?" he asked.

"Jeff Tennant."

Bill Wimple chuckled good-naturedly. "What makes you think Tennant would be here?" he inquired.

"Ye witless ape — is he or ain't he?" McGonigle demanded.

Then, seeing Mayme Shay on the upstairs landing, Tay called, "If Jeff is up there go tell him they're on their way here to get him!"

Jeff Tennant heard that. He watched Jane as she placed a compress on his wound, knowing that she had heard it also. But he saw no change in her face. It had held a strictly impersonal expression since the moment she'd entered this room and said, "Dad is away, Jeff. I'll do what I can."

Now as Mayme came in, closely followed by Hobo Bill, Tennant said, "I'll have to get out of here, right quick."

197

"But where will you go?" Mayme asked nervously. Tennant had no answer for that. "I'll figure it out after I leave," he muttered.

"You're in no shape to ride," Jane said, bandaging the wound as she talked and keeping her eyes on the task. "Even if you were, they're watching Bar Bell."

She finished tying the bandage and turned away, not looking as he reached for his pants. Hobo Bill helped him into them, saying, "I know a place you could hide, Jeff — and it wouldn't be far to walk."

"Where?" Tennant asked, buckling on his gun belt.

"The Bonanza Bazaar. Most of the roof has fell in, but Mayme's old dressing room is still in good shape. I was there the other day, sort of rememberin' old times."

"Just the place!" Mayme declared. "It's at the southwest corner of the building, Jeff. You can go in the back way from the alley."

Tennant stood up, balancing against the wobbly weakness of his knees. He glanced at Jane and found her gaze fully on him, and couldn't identify her expression. Gravity masked her mouth so that her lips were straight and inexpressive. But there was a change in the way she looked at him. Her lamplit eyes weren't coolly impersonal now. Nor calculating. There was an expression in them he had never seen before.

He said, "Thanks for saving my leg," and

hoped she would smile, wanting that much to re-member.

But she didn't smile. She said whisperingly, "I'd do as much for —"

Her voice seemed to fail, whereupon Tennant said, "For a dog," and made his own bitter reck-oning of the expression in her eyes. Disgust. He thought, *She despises me,* and wondered how this could be so.

She stood by the doorway with her face averted as he went out, passing so close that her hair made a distinct and familiar fragrance for him. He had a queerly thrusting impulse to take her head in his hands — to bury his face in the fluffy softness of her sorrel hair.

Hobo Bill followed Tennant from the room. "I'll bring you a blanket and a bait of grub," he promised, "soon's the coast is clear."

Tennant limped to the stairway, keeping his eyes on the front door. Perspiration dripped from his armpits as he descended the stairs, a step at a time. He heard Mayme say, "Ruth, you'll be the sick one that Miss Medwick is doc-toring."

And Hobo Bill said, "If Sheriff Lambert comes snoopin', you be sure to act like you're ailin', Ruth. Ailin' real bad."

Tennant limped through the kitchen where the tantalizing odor of fresh-boiled coffee re-minded him of how long it had been since he'd eaten. When he went outside the crisp night air was like a cold wave breaking against him. He had felt hot and feverish in the house; now, as he moved cautiously across the dark yard, he clenched his teeth to keep them from chattering. There'd been no snow south of Commissary Creek this afternoon, yet the west wind was so bitter cold now that Tennant turned up his mackinaw collar to protect his ears.

Turning into Sashay Alley, Tennant probed the dark thoroughfare for sign of traffic. All the lamplit windows were on the south side of the alley, its north side consisting of backyards behind Main Street's business establishments. He stood close to an adobe wall and watched a Mexican plod past with his blanket-wrapped shoulders hunched against the wind. Then Tennant crossed the alley and was into the Bonanza Bazaar's rubble-littered rear doorway when three men came along the dirt sidewalk.

Lambert and two deputies, Tennant thought instantly. He stepped to one side of the doorway; he stood there while the three men passed, and heard Clark Morgan say, "I'll watch the back door, Sam."

Sardonic amusement twisted Tennant's lips. Jane's husband-to-be didn't want her to see him. Morgan, he guessed, would be embarrassed to meet Jane in such a place; he would resent her going there even on a mission of mercy.

Tennant felt his way through the Bazaar's wreckage of fallen beams, wincing as his wounded leg bumped against a section of capsized roof. And at this moment, with his leg

200

hurting at each step, he remembered the poem Jane had quoted: *Rebels ride proudly in the sun, counting the battle already won.*

Well, he wasn't riding proudly now. He was limping through dark places like a chased coyote. And Jane despised him. That, he thought grimly, was the worst defeat of all. And the most astonishing. It had never occurred to him that Jane could despise him; that she would look at him as though the sight of him sickened her.

Tennant collided with a crumbling partition. He cursed, and lit a match, and saw a sagging door with a faded star painted on its warped boards.

"The star's dressing room," he reflected, absently holding the match until it burned his fingers. "Well, I'm the star, by God."

Cobwebs clung to his face as he went inside and sat on a dusty couch that creaked under his weight. The musty odor of mildew and mould and rain-soaked rubbish was trapped in this ancient room. He wondered how it had been in the old days when Mayme Shay changed gowns here and Hobo Bill came to pay his respects. The smells had been different then. There'd been perfume, and powder, and the fine feminine scent of a woman's hair. But now there was mildew and the mournful wail of the wind prowling through an abandoned place.

"Rebels ride proudly," Tennant muttered, and laughed, and sat there in the dark with his head in his hands.

22. "Because I Hate Him!"

Clark Morgan was waiting at the back door when Sheriff Lambert came out and said, "Tennant ain't in there. We searched every room, and he ain't there."

"What about Jane?" Morgan asked. "Is she taking care of a sick girl?"

Goldie Rimbaugh had come around through the yard in time to hear this. He said, "She didn't look sick to me. She looked fitter'n a fiddle, layin' there in that nice soft bed."

"How did she look to you, Sam?" Morgan asked.

"Healthy as a heifer," Lambert said. "She didn't have her sportin' paint on, so she was a trifle pale. But she sure didn't look like she was ailin'. When I asked what was wrong with her Miss Jane just shrugged and said she wasn't sure."

"Mebbe she's mournin' for old Dude," Rimbaugh suggested joshingly. "Dude used to call on her whenever he was in town."

Then Rimbaugh glanced up at the shed roof, which ran along the rear of the house. "If you'll give me a boost I'll go up there and take a looksee," he offered.

"Good idea," Morgan said. He helped Rimbaugh reach the roof and watched the TU rider negotiate its slanting, shingled surface on hands and knees.

Rimbaugh crept up to a window where lamp-light showed beneath a curtain that wasn't entirely lowered. He remained there for fully five minutes before coming back and dropping to the ground.

"What did you see?" Morgan asked.

Rimbaugh chuckled. "I saw plenty," he bragged, and smacked his lips. "She's no more sick than I be. She's sittin' up on the bed with her long white legs crossed sporty as you please, readin' a book."

"Is Miss Medwick with her?" Morgan asked.

Rimbaugh shook his head. "The blond is all alone, and she's wearin' the fanciest red rosebud garters I ever saw. She sure looks elegant, sprawled out there all alone."

Morgan said impatiently, "That means just one thing to me, Sam. My hunch was right. Mayme Shay came to get Doc for Tennant. But Tennant was warned and got out ahead of us."

Goldie Rimbaugh kept glancing up at the window. "How about me stayin' here, in case Tennant should come back?" he asked.

"No," Morgan decided with a tone of authority. "You go with Sheriff Sam and take a look at McGonigle's Livery. Tennant could have made it there while we've been here. I'll wait for Jane."

Lambert started off with Rimbaugh. Then he stopped and said, "You ought to have a gun, just in case."

"Couldn't hit anything if I had one," Morgan

muttered. He walked around the house and stood near the front veranda where the wind couldn't get at him. When Jane came out he tipped his hat and said censuringly, "Never thought I'd have to wait outside this place for you, dear."

Jane showed no surprise, taking his arm and walking with her head tipped against the wind.

"How's the sick girl?" Morgan asked casually. "Not very sick," Jane admitted. "Let's hurry, Clark. It's so cold."

"A bad night to be out," Morgan said. Then he asked, "Is Tennant badly wounded?" and watched her face.

Jane glanced at him, showing a brief disappointment before she said, "He's shot in the leg."

"So Tennant had you come to a parlor house to doctor him!" Morgan exclaimed with more passion than Jane had ever before heard in his voice. "What a disgraceful, degrading thing to involve my future wife in such a place!"

Jane asked quietly, "Are you ashamed of your future wife, Clark?"

"Of course not. But I resent Tennant dragging you to a parlor house."

"He sent for Dad," Jane explained. "He was quite surprised to see me, and not very pleased."

Presently Morgan asked, "Where did he go?"

Jane didn't answer for a moment. They were passing the Bonanza Bazaar's roofless walls when she asked, "You hate him, don't you, Clark?"

Then, not waiting for an answer, she said,

"Jeff didn't tell me where he was going. He just limped outside, with his hand close to his gun. I felt sorry for him, Clark. He looked so — so beaten and alone. I think he realizes now that there's no chance of Bar Bell winning."

"He doesn't deserve sympathy," Morgan muttered. "No decent person would do the things he's done."

"That's not why you hate him," Jane said. "Tate Usher has done things that weren't decent, and so has Idaho Cleek. But you don't hate them, do you, Clark?"

He made no reply, and presently Jane said, "It's because Jeff slapped you."

Morgan nodded. He halted and pulled her against him and said urgently, "I should have hit him back. But I knew he could whip me, and I couldn't bear to have you see him do it. I'll never forgive him for that slap. I've lain awake nights, thinking about it, and despising myself for not fighting back."

"You couldn't help it," Jane murmured. "You couldn't fight any more than Jeff could keep from fighting. It's the difference in the way you two are made, and in the way you've lived. Jeff has had to fight in order to survive. You've had to think and figure for a living. Don't you see, Clark?"

"No," Morgan said, calmness returning to his voice. "All I see is that Jeff Tennant tried to force me into a fight I couldn't win, for no other purpose than to belittle me in front of you."

"Poor Clark," Jane mused, walking close to him.

"Why do you say that?" Morgan demanded. "Because you need revenge so terribly, and there's no way for you to get it."

"There'd be a way, if I could find Tennant tonight," Morgan announced. "I'd slap him back, Jane — and keep on slapping him."

That surprised Jane, and she turned to peer at his face, asking, "Because he's wounded?"

"Because I hate him," Morgan muttered.

They were at Jane's front gate now. Tate Usher and Idaho Cleek rode up from the bridge and Usher asked, "Any sign of Tennant?"

"He's in town," Morgan said, very positive about this. "It's just a matter of smoking him out."

Jane said, "Good night, Clark," and walked to the veranda and heard Usher exclaim, "Then we'll get him, by God, if it takes all night!"

Some time during the night Jeff Tennant awoke to find a lighted candle burning in a tin can beside his couch. For a moment he couldn't orient himself; then he saw the bottle of whiskey on the floor and became aware of the patchwork quilt that covered him.

"Hobo Bill kept his promise," Tennant thought aloud.

When he reached for the bottle he lost his balance and fell off the couch, taking the quilt with him. He loosed a groaning curse and lay there for a time with his lips tight pressed while successive splinters of pain clawed at his wounded leg. The floor was damp, its coldness soaking into him. He thought, *I've got to get up,* and dreaded to move his wounded leg, and decided to take a drink first. When he picked up the quart bottle it seemed heavy but he saw that it was less than half full.

"I'm weak as a gutted rabbit," he muttered, and took a drink.

The whiskey was cold to his mouth, but it felt warm in his stomach. Presently he drank again and was sweating when he got back onto the couch. Afterward he noticed the paper-wrapped sandwich on the floor. Bracing himself against the dizziness that came each time he moved, Tennant picked up the sandwich — thick beef, which he ate with relish. Then he took another long pull at the bottle and blew out the candle.

A whimpering wind ran through the Bazaar. The sound of it made Tennant shiver. He pulled the quilt up around his ears and wondered what time it was. Must be close to daylight, he reckoned, and decided to stay awake. But he was sound asleep when Jane came in and said, "Wake up, Jeff."

It was daylight now and Tennant blinked his eyes, scarcely believing what he saw; for Jane was offering him a sack of doughnuts and a fruit jar filled with hot coffee.

"How do you feel?" she inquired.

"Good, now," Tennant announced. He took the coffee and doughnuts, asking, "Would the girl also do this for a dog?"

"The girl didn't say that," Jane insisted, and watched him eat for a moment before adding, "I meant I'd do as much for you any time."

"You meant that?" Tennant demanded.

Jane nodded. "I felt so bad I couldn't quite finish saying it."

"Then you don't despise me," Tennant mused, and let the pleasure of that knowledge show in his happy smile.

"Where did you get that notion?" Jane demanded.

"At Mayme Shay's. You scarcely glanced at me. You looked as if the sight of me made you sick."

"It did, Jeff, to think how high a price you'd paid for — for nothing," Jane said gently. "You were wounded and had no place to go. You couldn't even stay at Mayme's. I thought about that after I went to bed. Every time the wind howled I thought of you with a wounded leg in this cold place."

"Then it was pity I saw in your eyes," Tennant decided. He glanced at the diamond ring on her left hand and said, "So you're going to marry Clark Morgan."

"On the fifteenth," Jane murmured. "You'll be gone by then."

"Gone where?"

"You'll leave Bunchgrass Basin, won't you — soon as you're able to ride?"

And when Tennant shook his head, Jane asked

urgently, "But how can you stay in a country where there's a reward for your capture, dead or alive?"

"How much reward?" Tennant asked, curious about this.

"One hundred dollars, put up by the county."

A mocking grin slanted Tennant's darkly bearded cheeks. "They don't place a very high value on my hide," he reflected, and was drinking the last of his coffee when Clark Morgan stepped into the room.

"Clark!" Jane cried.

Morgan didn't look at her but came directly to the couch. He said in a queerly breathless voice, "Damn you!" and struck Tennant in the face.

Surprise, and a sense of utter disbelief, ran through Jeff Tennant. He dropped the fruit jar and tried to kick free of the cumbersome quilt, but Morgan pounced on him instantly, pounding at his face with both fists. One of Morgan's knees made an intolerable grinding pressure against Tennant's wounded leg. Jeff grunted a curse and put all his strength into a desperate attempt to push Morgan back, but the merchant clubbed him with a hard right to the temple.

Tennant fell back. He tried to target Morgan's fiercely scowling face. His eyes didn't focus properly and he missed, and thought, *Here's where I take a licking.* Then something seemed to explode against his face. A tremendous burst of dazzling light blinded him and there was a queer, rhythmic throbbing in his ears. After that, for a time, there was nothing at all. . . .

When Tennant opened his eyes he saw Jane's tear-stained face and wondered why she had been crying. He got up on an elbow, groggily shaking his head. He wiped his bleeding lips on an up-hunched shoulder, peered about the room and asked, "When did Morgan leave?"

"Just now," Jane said in an emotion-choked voice.

Tennant considered her for a moment, sensing the change in her. She seemed hysterical and bewildered. There was a startled expression in her eyes as she came over to the couch and explored his bruised face with gentle fingers, asking, "Do you feel all right?"

Tennant nodded, and was aware of whiskey's pungent odor. Then he noticed that her right sleeve was wet to the elbow. The thought that came to him now seemed so ridiculous that he rejected it at once. Yet even as he refused to accept such a fantastic explanation, Jane said worriedly, "I can't understand why I hit him."

Tennant grasped her by the shoulders. "You mean you hit Morgan with the whiskey bottle?" he demanded.

Jane nodded. She said soberly, "I don't remember picking it up. Clark was pounding you — and you weren't fighting back. Then I hit him on the head with the bottle. It was awful, Jeff. He fell down and groaned, and I thought I'd killed him."

A spasmodic hoot of gusty laughter burst from Tennant. "You hit Morgan with a bottle!" he exclaimed. Then he tilted back on the couch and laughed until tears coursed down his fist-scarred face.

"It's not funny," Jane objected.

"You hit Morgan!" Tennant gasped gleefully and let laughter claim him again.

"Stop laughing at me!" Jane protested.

But now she was laughing too, so Tennant said, "I'm not laughing at you, honey — I'm laughing with you!"

23. A Delicacy Long Delayed

Tay McGonigle was watering horses at the livery trough when Doc Medwick drove up shortly after eight o'clock.

"How's things at Bar Bell?" Tay inquired, taking charge of Doc's horse.

Medwick got down and stamped his feet. "Terrible," he muttered. "Huffmeyer has a concussion, Lunsford's arm is broken and Shakespear Smith froze both his feet."

"How about Kid Peebles?" Tay asked.

"He died at four o'clock this morning," Doc said wearily. "Did they catch Jeff Tennant?"

The liveryman shook his head. "But they damn near did, thanks to pussyfootin' Clark Morgan. Jeff is in town some place, but they ain't found him yet."

"Good," Doc said. "I got here in time."

"Time for what?"

"To call off the law dogs that are chasing him," Medwick said and walked hurriedly to the sheriff's office.

"You," Doc greeted, peering at Lambert, "look like I feel."

"Up all night huntin' that stinkin' son Tennant," Lambert said sourly.

"Then you wasted your time," Doc announced and slumped into a chair. "Tennant didn't kill Red Naviska."

"Who says?" Lambert demanded.

"The same one who said he did — Johnny Peebles. Johnny knew he was dying. He got scared toward the last — like a kid afraid of the dark. Just before he died Johnny told me how he shot Naviska, mistaking him for Petty. He said Cleek and Usher put him up to saying it was Tennant. They told him he'd hang, otherwise."

Lambert loosed a long sigh. A grin rutted his beard-stubbled jaws and he said, "So now I've got no legal reason for arrestin' Tennant, by God."

"None at all," Medwick muttered. He eyed Lambert thoughtfully for a moment before saying, "You've kept Tate Usher on your blind side all along, Sam. He's the one who needed arresting."

Lambert bristled at once. "What you mean?" he demanded. "What's Usher done that I could arrest him for? He ain't killed nobody!"

"No, Sam, but I'm convinced he framed Jeff Tennant into prison. He tried a similar trick on Ben Petty, making it look as if Ed Peebles was murdered. And now we know the Naviska deal against Jeff was a frame-up."

The sheriff frowningly considered Doc's summation. "But I still ain't got legal cause to arrest Usher," he said defensively.

"Perhaps not," Doc admitted. "But you've got to release your TU deputies, and do it quick. Is Usher in town?"

Lambert nodded. He scowled, not liking this

at all. "That means tellin' Tate about Kid Peebles' confession. And Tate'll deny it, sure as hell."

Medwick got up, walked to the door and turned, saying, "You'll have no moral right to interfere with Jeff, when the showdown comes."

"What showdown?"

"The day Jeff goes after Usher with a gun."

Lambert grimaced. "Bein' sheriff durin' a range war is a poor way to earn the groceries," he complained.

"I know of a worse way," Doc said, without sympathy.

"What?"

"Being a doctor during a range war," Medwick muttered and was facing the door when Clark Morgan opened it.

The merchant was pale and excited. He took off his hat and showed Doc a bruise and asked, "Does it need your attention?"

Doc fingered it, finally shaking his head. "How'd you get it?"

"You would never guess," Morgan said,

"Jeff Tennant?" Medwick asked.

"Well, yes, in a way of speaking," Morgan admitted, and turned to Lambert, saying, "You can go get Tennant at the Bonanza Bazaar. He won't give you any trouble. I knocked him out."

"You knocked Jeff Tennant out?" Lambert blurted.

"Yes," Morgan said and contrived a bragging

tone that was convincing. "I knocked him out cold."

Lambert put on his coat and walked with Medwick into Sashay Alley. When they reached the Bazaar's rear doorway the sound of laughter led them to the dressing room.

Doc Medwick sniffed the whiskey-laden air. He peered suspiciously at Jane and demanded, "What's the joke?"

Tennant pushed Jane away from him. He said sharply, "You're not arresting me, Lambert," and had his gun half drawn when Doc announced, "There's no charge against you, Jeff. Kid Peebles confessed to Naviska's killing!"

"So," Tennant mused. He looked at Medwick, not thoroughly convinced, and asked, "Then what's Lambert doing here?"

"Sam is going to see that you reach my house without being bothered by his TU deputies," Doc said.

Lambert glanced at the whiskey bottle on the floor. "Is that what Morgan knocked you out with?" he asked.

"Why, no," Tennant said. "Morgan is too much of a gentleman to use anything but his fists."

Jane laughed. She took Tennant's arm and said, "Let's go home, Jeff. Your bandage needs changing."

Which was when Doc Medwick noticed that the diamond ring was missing from his daughter's left hand. . . .

★ ★ ★

For five days, while Tennant loafed on the parlor lounge, Jane spent most of her time in the kitchen, preparing such bounteous meals that Doc said teasingly, "Anyone would think you were trying to get Jeff fat enough to kill off." And Jane, who'd never been more cheerful, said evenly, "Perhaps that's what it amounts to."

On the third day Bravo Shafter had called to ask about Tennant's condition and to say that Leona, who was nursing three injured men, couldn't leave Bar Bell but that she would like to see him as soon as he could ride.

"Tell her I won't be coming back to Bar Bell," Tennant said. "The ramrod job is all yours, Bravo."

Then, while they were eating their noon meal on the fifth day, Tennant said casually, "Guess it's about time I moved to the hotel."

"What's the rush?" Doc asked. "Doesn't Jane's cooking suit you?"

"Best meals I've ever eaten," Tennant declared, smiling at Jane. "It's just that I've always made it a practice not to ride grubline at one place too long. Wears out your welcome."

But Jane wasn't fooled at all. She said quietly, "You want to be where you can watch Usher when he comes to town."

"Usher and Cleek are in town now," Doc reported. Seeing the swift frown on Jane's face, he asked, "Did you see them ride past, Jeff?"

"Yeah," Tennant said. "I saw them."

Then, without looking at Jane, he got up from the table. He went into the hall, put on his hat and mackinaw and went quickly outside.

The sunless air was damp and cold, but there was no wind. Tennant limped to the gate and opened it, the hinges creaking loudly. When he closed the gate he saw Jane's face at the kitchen window. He waved, and carried the picture of her wistful smile with him as he tromped the road's frozen mud.

When Tennant came to Biddle's barbershop he peered through the front window to see Windy comfortably enthroned in the barber's chair. A thin smile edged Tennant's lips; he thought, *Windy will like this,* and stepped inside, saying, "Go tell Tate Usher to come out on the street so I can get a shot at him."

Biddle's eyes bugged wide. "You — you mean it?" he demanded.

Tennant nodded, and when the barber made no move to go, Tennant said sharply, "Go tell him."

"Sure," Biddle agreed excitedly. He started out the door, then came back for his derby. "Judas priest!" he exclaimed and ran out and said again, "Judas priest!"

Tennant stood in the doorway. When Biddle hurried into the Palace Saloon there was no movement on Main Street until Tay McGonigle came out of the hotel and walked toward the livery, picking his teeth. Recalling how disappointed the little Irishman had been at missing out on the Stromberg fight, Tennant was tempted to tell him what was coming. But it occurred to Tennant that if Idaho Cleek made this a two-to-one showdown Tay would get no pleasure from witnessing it.

Tennant watched the Palace. He thought, *Maybe Usher won't come out. Maybe I'll have to go in after him.*

Doc Medwick came along the plank walk, carrying his black satchel. He said gravely, "Good luck, Jeff," and went on toward the Senate Hotel without stopping.

Perspiration greased the palm of Tennant's right hand. He wiped it on his pants and swore morosely, knowing what a long wait would do to his nerves. A man's imagination always got the best of him at a time like this. It made him go through a fight several times before the fight started. It pulled his nerves too tight, and put butterflies in his belly.

Tennant wiped his palm again. He said, "To hell with waiting," and limped across the street's frozen clods.

He was within twenty feet of the Palace when Tate Usher stepped through the batwings and stopped on the stoop's front edge. "You looking for me?" Usher called.

Tennant halted at once. He said, "Yes," and eyed Usher with a rising wonderment. Tate was alone, and yet he seemed wholly confident, almost careless, in the way he stood there blandly smiling.

"Well, here I am," Usher announced, the words sliding into sly laughter.

The effect of that laugh on Tennant was like flame igniting powder. All the contempt and all the hatred of three long years fused into an itching urge to kill. Anticipation now was a gnawing hunger; a raw wild eagerness rasped his voice when he shouted, "Draw, damn you — draw!"

But instead of grabbing his gun, Usher glanced sideways, and Tennant did likewise — to see Idaho Cleek standing at the saloon's west corner.

So that's how it's to be, Tennant thought, and understood why Usher appeared so confident. This was as it always had been — two to one. Usher and Cleek, mostly Cleek. It would never be otherwise. Even here on Main Street, with spectators to witness his yellow-cored cowardice, Tate Usher wouldn't fight alone. . . .

A sighing curse slid from Tennant's lips. The thought came to him that he had a choice here: that he could honorably withdraw from so unfair a fight. But there'd never be a better deal; never be a time when the deck wasn't stacked against him.

"Well?" Usher taunted.

As if impatient of delay TU's boss reached for his gun with such deliberate slowness that Tennant thought fleetingly, *He's forcing me to draw, but Cleek will do the shooting!*

Tennant snatched his gun from holster.

Ignoring Cleek he fired at Usher while the big man's clumsy draw was being completed, slamming three bullets into that broad target and seeing it flounder sideways across the stoop. Then he looked at Cleek.

For a hushed interval astonishment had its way with Jeff Tennant. The TU ramrod leaned indolently against the saloon wall, thumbs hooked into gun belt. He hadn't drawn and he showed no intention of drawing now. Tennant waited not quite sure and wanting to be sure — wanting to know why Cleek had double-crossed his boss. Tate Usher had expected Cleek to do the shooting; Usher had been so sure of it that he'd forced a showdown deliberately. And Cleek had let Usher die without lifting a hand in his defense.

Doc Medwick hurried over to the Palace stoop and knelt beside Usher's sprawled body. Big Sid Stromberg came out and stared at Idaho Cleek as if seeing him for the first time.

"What in hell happened?" Stromberg asked.

Cleek nodded at Tennant and said dryly, "He was too fast for Tate."

"But how about you?" the saloonman demanded.

"Wasn't my fight," Cleek muttered. "Tate tried to outdraw Tennant, and didn't do it."

But that didn't explain the deal to Stromberg. Nor to Tennant. There was something more to it than that; something that had caused Idaho Cleek to double-cross his boss. . . .

Lee Pardee and Goldie Rimbaugh stood in front of Vedder's shop, Pardee supporting a re-lined saddle on one shoulder and exclaiming, "Usher got it hisself, by God! He finally got it!"

Tennant holstered his gun. He had not taken his eyes from Cleek, and now called, "You're through in Bunchgrass Basin, and you're leaving the country."

"No," Cleek said. "I ain't through and I ain't leaving."

A mirthless smile briefly altered the composed set of his dark features as he added, "Tate and me owned TU together, Tennant. Now I own it alone."

That astonished Tennant. "You'll need proof," he declared. "Legal proof."

"I've got it," Cleek declared, a bragging insolence in his voice. "The partnership paper was signed and witnessed by Judge Maffit. It's in a sealed envelope at the courthouse."

"So that's it," Tennant said thoughtfully, as understanding came to him. "That's why you didn't side Usher."

Cleek shrugged, not bothering to deny this, and Tennant recalled another incident that had puzzled him and that now was easily explained: Idaho's warning at Nugget Wash. Cleek had refrained from dry-gulching him so that he might live to do what he'd done today — kill Tate Usher.

"The partnership paper doesn't change things," Tennant said stubbornly. "I'm giving you one day's time to get out."

Cleek peered at Tennant for a long moment, as if teetering on the thin edge of a showdown here and now. Finally he said, "I own TU and it'll take a good gun to drive me off it."

Then Cleek walked to his horse at the saloon hitchrack, climbed into saddle and rode down Main Street. When he passed Jane Medwick at the feed store he said, "No use to hurry, ma'am. Shootin's all over."

"Who won?" Jane asked breathlessly.

Cleek halted his horse. "Tennant," he said, and seeing her relief, added a cryptic warning, "Tennant won't be so lucky next time. You'd better get that into his thick head."

He rode on then, and Jane hurried into town, wanting to see Jeff; wanting to touch him and to know that he was all right. There was a crowd in front of the Palace. She saw Jeff standing off to one side with Goldie Rimbaugh and Lee Pardee; when she came close she heard Jeff say, "You boys been lucky up to now. Get out before your luck changes."

"Sure," Rimbaugh agreed. "I've saw enough."

They moved off and Jane hurried to Tennant, her flushed face smiling and her eyes brightly shining. But all she said was, "Jeff!"

The news of Tate Usher's death ran the length and breadth of Quadrille within an hour. By suppertime it was the topic of conversation in Fremont Street homes and in the adobe huts of

Sashay Alley. If anyone regretted Usher's sudden demise there was no mention of it publicly. Jeff Tennant was the town's hero not so much for winning a gun duel with Usher as for his brash ultimatum to Idaho Cleek.

"I always knowed Jeff could beat Cleek," Billy Barlow bragged. "Cleek knows it too, or he'd of drawed against Jeff."

This was in the hotel dining room and within hearing of Clark Morgan who was eating supper with Sheriff Lambert. "Gun talk," Morgan complained. "That's all you hear. You would think that killing a man with a bullet was the pinnacle of success the way people are praising Tennant. But I say he has no right to force Cleek off the land Idaho now owns. Gun might doesn't make legal right."

"Well," Lambert said, "gun might made TU. All Usher's land grabs was within the law, but it was gun might that put 'em over."

Even Effie Barlow felt differently about Tennant, for now, as she served Sheriff Lambert, she said, "Jeff certainly changed things all around, killing Usher like he did. It'll be all right for Ben Petty to come back, won't it, Sam?"

"Any time," Lambert assured her. "Any time at all."

Effie smiled. "I'll write to Rose tonight," she said. "It'll be so nice to have her home again."

"She won't be back here," Joe Barlow predicted. "She'll be with her husband in the Tailholt Hills. And we'll be up there too, soon's we sell this damned hotel."

"But suppose Idaho Cleek stays at TU," Effie argued.

"He won't," young Billy declared, "I'll bet he's on his way out right now, just like Jeff told him. Look how Pardee and Rimbaugh left, not even waitin' to git their wages."

"I know," Effie said, "but there's nothing to stop Cleek from hiring more men."

Which was approximately what Jeff Tennant was trying to tell Doc at the Medwick supper table while Jane listened attentively. . . .

"I fought Usher because he framed me into prison," Tennant explained, "but I've got a better reason for fighting Cleek."

"What?" Medwick asked.

Tennant looked at Jane, a mute question in his eyes.

Jane nodded. She said thoughtfully, "It's because Cleek was Usher's club over the small outfits, and there'll be no chance for men like Joe Barlow and Ben Petty while Cleek remains at TU. That's your reason, isn't it, Jeff?"

"Yes," Tennant said, and smiled at her, and thought, *She's lovelier right now than she's ever been.*

Afterward, when Doc had gone off for his evening poker game and the dishes were put away, Tennant sat on the parlor lounge with Jane close beside him. "The man," he said, "has a confession to make. But first he wants to kiss the girl."

"So?" Jane prompted.

Tennant took her in his arms. He supported her head, tilting it so that the lamp on the piano lighted her eyes. "The exact color of campfire smoke," he whispered, and kissed them in turn. Then he kissed her ears, and her chin and the soft white hollow of her throat.

He lifted his head, rashly smiling, and looked at her lips. But he made no move to kiss them and so Jane asked, "Haven't you forgotten one important place?"

Tennant shook his head. "I'm saving it till last," he said with a boyish grin. "Until after the confession."

Then, reverting to the sober tone he'd used to introduce this subject, he said, "The man did wrong, signing up to fight Usher for a hundred cows and five bulls. He had no right allowing the Barlows to risk their lives helping him win such a prize. His best girl didn't like it and she told him so, but he was too stubborn to see it her way. He kept trying to win, but the Lord was on the girl's side and the man lost the prize. But he won the girl — a girl who hits her prospective husbands with whiskey bottles and knocks 'em cold."

Then, while her lips were sweetly curved with low laughter, Tennant kissed them in the fashion of a man relishing a delicacy long delayed.

24. Gunhawk's Harvest

Jeff Tennant awoke to find sunlight streaming in the window of his hotel room. He got up at once, liking this first sight of the sun in a week. He was pulling on his boots when he remembered what he had told Idaho Cleek.

One day's time. . . .

And remembered telling Jane that he would start for TU about noon. "Cleek," he'd said, "will probably be gone before I get there."

But Jane had said, "You don't believe that," and when he left she had promised gravely, "I shall pray for you, Jeff."

Billy Barlow came in with a pitcher of hot water. "Ma says she's got a presentment that Cleek will be waitin' for you to run him off TU," the boy announced. "You reckon she's right, Jeff?"

"She might be," Tennant admitted. "Women seem to know about such things."

He went to the washstand, limping a trifle, and Billy asked, "Is your leg healed enough so's you can ride?"

Tennant nodded, knowing what was in Billy's mind. He washed his face and combed his hair while Billy watched. When he buckled on his gun belt the boy asked, "You goin' to ride out there this afternoon?"

"Yeah," Tennant said.

They went down to breakfast, Billy sharing Tennant's table and not speaking until the meal was over. Then, as Tennant took out his Durham sack, Billy inquired secretively, "Do you ever git scairt before a gun fight, Jeff?"

Tenant nodded.

That seemed to surprise Billy. He peered at Tennant's steady fingers rolling the cigarette. "You don't act the least bit nervous," he said. "You didn't look scairt when you faced Usher and Cleek yesterday."

"It doesn't show on the outside," Tennant explained. "It's a feeling inside you, deep down."

Billy thought about this for a moment in squint-eyed silence. "Like the way I always feel before I git onto a bronc that's sure to pitch?" he asked. "A sort of all-gone feelin'?"

"Yeah," Tennant said. "Just like that."

"Gosh," Billy mused, and grinned, and exclaimed, "I didn't think anybody else ever got that kind of scairt feelin' but me!"

"Everyone gets it," Tennant assured him. "They don't talk about it, is all."

Afterward, when Tennant went over to the livery and asked Tay McGonigle if he could buy a team of horses on credit, the little Irishman said, "Ye can, bejasus and a good wagon to go with them. Ye figgerin' to build a new cabin at Roman Four?"

Tennant nodded, then asked, "Did that Bar Bell horse come here after I turned it loose at Mayme's the other night?"

227

"Nope — must of gone back to the ranch."

"Then I'll need to borrow a horse and saddle for this afternoon," Tennant said.

"Consider it done, although I think ye'll be awastin' of your time ridin' out there, Jeff. It's in me mind that Cleek has high-tailed for the tules, after the way he acted yesterday. Ye would of thought he was a North-of-Ireland dude runnin' from a banshee."

This seemed to be the consensus of opinion among Quadrille's menfolks. But when Tennant called on Mayme Shay to thank her and Hobo Bill for their fine favors, Mayme insisted on fixing him a steak so rare that blood oozed from it. "You'll need strength and courage when you face Idaho Cleek," she declared. "The dirty devil will fight like a cornered rat."

And that, although he tried not to think about it, was how Tennant expected it would be. Cleek had side-stepped yesterday believing there was a chance to wait it out. Considering this, Tennant guessed there might be another reason: Idaho had a reputation for fast and accurate shooting, but in all the time he'd been in Bunchgrass Basin Cleek hadn't drawn against a man who was also fast and accurate.

Maybe I looked real good against Usher yesterday, Tennant thought and felt a rising confidence. Cleek might not be quite as nerveless as he appeared to be. . . .

At one o'clock Tennant rode slowly past Doc Medwick's house. Jane didn't come out, or show

228

herself at a window, which seemed odd. He glanced back once, expecting to see her come running out to the gate. But there was no sign of Jane.

Disappointment seeped coldly through Tennant, yet presently he muttered, "It's better this way," and felt a sense of relief. Jane had been close to tears when they parted last night. Perhaps that was why she hadn't come out to wish him luck.

Recalling the fine evening they'd had together, Tennant smiled reflectively. Jane was wearing his ring now. An engagement ring. But there was no diamond in it, for it was fashioned from a horseshoe nail. They'd made new plans together, deciding to build their house a section at a time. First would come a one-room cabin which would be the kitchen. Afterward they could add a large parlor and a bedroom.

"Poco a poco," Jane had said smilingly, which was the Mexican way of saying little by little.

Tennant grinned, remembering how he'd once refused to consider marriage until he had a fitting home for his bride — and how easily Jane had talked him out of that idea last night. "We'll share a shack of dreams," she'd said, "and build it into a home." But mostly she had talked him out of it with her eyes and the frank, sweet pressure of her lips. . . .

There wasn't enough warmth in the sunlight to thaw the frozen mud. Ice rimmed the edges of Commissary Creek at the crossing and a thin coating of snow covered Tonto Flats. Tennant saw several TU steers, some of them pawing at snow-shrouded grass and all of them ribby gaunt. He got to thinking about the ill-fated drive, and what a huge difference that failure had brought. If the steer drive had succeeded he would still be Bar Bell's ramrod, Jane wouldn't have broken her engagement to Clark Morgan, and Tate Usher would be alive. It seemed ironical that a shift in the wind could have caused such radical changes in the lives of so many people.

Tennant quartered into the Tailholt Hills, passing Ben Petty's shack and later pausing to consider the forlorn emptiness of Roman Four. He thought, *It'll look different a month from now,* and smiled, visualizing how the new cabin would look. There'd be fancy curtains at the windows, and all the little things inside by means of which a woman contrives to turn a house into a home. But mostly it would be Jane who'd make it different — Jane's warmly glowing eyes and soft lips, and the fine fragrance of her hair. It occurred to Tennant how much he stood to lose in a shoot out with Idaho Cleek; infinitely more than he'd ever lost before.

He was past Menafee Camp when he saw the rig ahead of him and recognized its occupants almost at once. Surprise ran its brief course while Jane and Doc Medwick looked back, their faces partly hidden by upturned coat collars. Why, he wondered, were they driving toward

TU, and had partly guessed the answer before Doc explained, "This was Jane's idea. She wanted me handy, in case you need some medical attention afterward."

"Then it's to be a duel with all the fixings," Tennant said, wanting to dispel the gravity that was like a dark veil on Jane's face.

She smiled up at him. "I know you'll win," she said with quiet confidence. "It's just that I want you patched up quick in case you're wounded so you can start work on our cabin tomorrow."

"No rest for the wicked," Tennant complained and leaned over in saddle to kiss her.

Presently Doc asked, "No chance to talk you out of it, is there, Jeff?"

Tennant shook his head, and Doc inquired nervously, "Think you can beat Cleek's draw?"

Tennant nodded. "We'll know for sure in a few minutes," he said and rode on at an easy lope, sitting tall and straight in the saddle.

Idaho Cleek came out of the office and peered at Baldy who stood in the bunkhouse doorway. "See anybody coming?" he called crankily.

"Not a sign," the cook said.

"Then go turn some dogs loose," Cleek ordered. "I ain't had any target practice for a week."

Baldy went to the pens, opened a gate and chased four male dogs into the yard. Then he stood close to a protecting corner of the cookshack while Cleek drew and fired. Idaho

231

missed the first dog, overshooting by a foot or more. He cursed, holstered his gun and tried again. The dog yelped once and collapsed, briefly threshing. Cleek killed the next two with swift, sure precision, missed the fourth which ran across the yard with its tail between its legs until Cleek knocked it over without seeming to take aim.

"Chouse out some more," Cleek ordered, reloading his gun.

"Ain't no more males," Baldy reported.

"To hell with males!" Cleek exclaimed. "Turn loose some dogs and be goddam quick about it!"

"Sure," Baldy said, not liking the queer, crazy look in Cleek's eyes. He hurried over to the pens and let out three females and noticed that one of them had a litter of pups. He tried to turn the mother back, but she got away and so did two of her wobbling puppies.

Baldy was closing the gate when he saw a rider cross the Rio Pago. He said at once, "Here comes Tennant!" But Cleek, already firing at the dogs, didn't hear him. A bullet struck the pups' mother. She fell, then got up, dragging one hind leg.

"Don't kill her!" Baldy protested. "She's got suckin' pups!"

Cleek laughed and fired again, killing the bitch as she crawled toward her fat, fluffy pups.

Baldy watched the puppies sniff at their dead mother. He said, "You shouldn't of killed her," and swore dejectedly as Cleek killed the pups with two shots.

"You're just a chicken-hearted old woman," Cleek jeered and reloaded his gun. "You ain't got guts enough in your goddam belly to fill a thimble."

"But them pups was real cute," Baldy muttered. He saw Tennant ride up behind the house — and saw the gun Tennant aimed at him.

"Don't stand there like a sniveling female," Cleek shouted impatiently. "Turn loose another batch of targets."

Baldy hurried to the pens and wondered if Tennant was going to shoot Cleek in the back. "Serve the dirty son right," the cook mumbled. He was opening the pen gate when he heard Tennant call sharply, "Make your play, Cleek!"

Baldy looked around, saw Cleek go stiff as a fence post. Idaho had his gun out. But Tennant was behind him and Idaho didn't move. He scowled at Baldy and accused, "You goddam double-crosser!"

Baldy shivered, and saw a rig out at the edge of the yard and was wondering about that when Tennant said, "Holster your gun and I'll do the same, Cleek. Then turn around and draw."

"Sure," Idaho agreed.

He started to holster his gun and Baldy saw Tennant do likewise. But then, with just the snout in leather, Cleek whirled. . . .

The rest of it was almost too fast for Baldy to watch. At the exact instant Cleek whirled and fired Tennant dropped flat on the ground. Then Tennant's gun exploded twice and Cleek's shoulders jerked each time. Cleek tripped over a dead dog; he fired one more shot as he went down, the bullet splashing mud a yard behind Tennant.

Tennant got up and contemplated Cleek's motionless shape for a moment. Presently he asked, "Was it a fair fight, Baldy?"

"Awful fair," the cook announced gustily. "Too goddam fair, in fact!"

Then Baldy watched Tennant limp across the yard to meet a girl who came running toward him. There were tears in the girl's eyes. But she was smiling.

"Jeff!" she cried. "Oh, Jeff!"